SHIBDEN
Love & Money

L.A.GREENAN

SHIBDEN LOVE & MONEY

First edition. August 1, 2023.

Written by L.A.Greenan.

Alex

2010 - 2022

may you forever be chasing birds

and eating toast.

Chapter One

HOME SWEET HOME

What's that age-old saying? You know, the one every woman says, and you think to yourself, that makes perfect sense, but you ignore them and do the opposite anyway. That's it! Trust your instincts and have no regrets. Well, perhaps Hannah should've, I mean, it's completely obvious to her now that she should've taken it on board from the very beginning of her marriage, but she didn't. And now she's left scared, like a wounded little lamb with the voices in her head saying, *'I bloody told you so!'*

Straightening the cushions on the sofa and brushing the dog hairs from the throw, Hannah attempted to push away the dark thoughts that crept into her mind.

'Hannah, you're your own worst enemy. You appear like an expensive painted doll on the outside but inside we see what you really are: used and unwanted. You're slowly breaking apart like a jigsaw puzzle. You're useless and unworthy.

Does anyone else have this constant internal dialogue? The internal battle to stop belittling herself was an ongoing one for her. Self-help books (she has many) tell you to make peace with yourself and learn to love yourself, but is this even possible? She can't seem to

1

shake the constant stream of thoughts and daydreams that haunt her, the overthinking mind of hers with what-ifs. How can she find a way to move past this? It's never ending.

She gazes out onto the Shibden Valley beneath her, the first golden daffodils of spring appearing out amongst the grey and weathered fields. Its beauty never failed to captivate her, no matter the season, but it still can't quiet the voices in her head. At least she has this view. The valley is a constant source of beauty that never lets her down. This year, it's been one of the few dependable things in her life; it brings feelings of warmth even to the coldest heart, and there's a lot of them around here.

The Burnside family's barn house has stood proudly facing the valley for two decades. This eco-friendly barn conversion features two floors, four bedrooms, and a garage large enough to fit a swimming pool. She stands in the open-plan living area with breath-taking views of the valley below, whose colours change like a kaleidoscope as the clouds pass by. Securing planning permission in this historic region is no easy task, but the Burnsides have a finger in everything and seem to have had no trouble securing this. Something she enjoyed in the early days; a power she wasn't used to and relished in, but as time passed, she began questioning things.

She has recently found herself reflecting on what could have been if things had gone differently, never knowing of his deceit. A vast array of "what ifs" but when she looks at the result, all she is left with is emptiness. The bitter cold of the Yorkshire stone beneath her well-manicured feet serves as a reminder of the twenty-year relationship that has been broken by betrayal. He had someone else, and the love and friendship they had shared for two decades is now gone, washed away like the red beck in the valley below.

The beeping of a horn at the front gate snaps her out of the daydream, and Hannah knows it's time to put her 'happy face' on. Looking in the full-length mirror, all she sees is her petite blond self, a shadow of who she once was, a glaze across her blue-grey eyes has now set in. It's especially difficult because the reason for his visit is to say farewell to Maggie, who had been like a mother to Hannah ever since she lost her own years ago. Maggie was a close family friend of Martha Burnside, Dylan's Mum, who had mentored Hannah on navigating the accounts department at Burnside Holdings - only for them both to be pushed aside by Maggie's arrogant son Richard.

Upon seeing Dylan Burnside, 'Mr magnificent' himself, 'King of the valley' who has returned briefly to the area, leave the taxi, her nerves set in. He doesn't even take a moment to acknowledge the taxi driver who shouts, 'I will wait, sir' as Dylan struts on down the drive. This infuriates Hannah, as it's typical of a Burnside to be so thoughtless.

As soon as she opens the door, it only takes a single whiff of Dylan's aftershave to take over her senses and all her strength melts away. He casts a glance over her, his wife, who was once his everything, whom he betrayed, and a look of sadness appears briefly before his expression hardens. Hannah knows that once he opens his mouth, his harsh words would break the spell, and she must remind herself to stay strong and stand her ground with him. "See you've smashed the gatepost on the bottom of drive again," he smirks. "Would it be the twenty point turn you did in the car the other day?" At this point, he will say anything just for her to speak to him.

"I'm sure you know the answer to that given the CCTV stalking you are prone to doing," replies Hannah. Their bickering has become childish. They pause for just second, and a look of longing crosses both their faces. But trying to be the adult here, Hannah steps aside to allow him to enter. His Italian leather boots thud as he walks through the front door.

Dylan's a tall man, standing at six feet two; with a full head of dark hair, now greying slightly, but looking incredibly good for his age. His golden eyes gaze around the room and he can't help but be impressed with the size of the open plan living space every time he enters it. It always made him feel small compared to his grand design. He designed this with his late father Jock 'The Gunner' Burnside. They spent months planning it so it could feel like a small part of Scotland in Yorkshire. Dylan's a proud Yorkshire man but never forgets his father's Scottish heritage which built the Burnside empire.

"So, Mum's pretty upset about Maggie's death, but she's determined to give her the best send-off, given they were best friends for years," he pipes up, still admiring the craftsmanship of his barn. He does his best not to keep staring at Hannah as he doesn't want her to see the pain, he tries to hide from her. He's well aware that Hannah is tired of hearing about Martha, the living she devil. Hannah rolls her eyes at him.

"Well, she didn't seem so bestie with her when Maggie was dealing with Richard running off and not telling her where the hell he is!"

"Forget Richard, he caused the company more trouble than I can mention, and Maggie was aware of that." He snaps back at her at the mention of Richard. "I'm sure your Mum will manage with her best boy by her side to help her." Hannah responds sarcastically. He doesn't answer her back and shouts towards the stairs, "Eva, are you ready, we need to go now, not next year! Move your arse."

Their only daughter, Eva, who had just come back from University for the funeral, didn't respond. She had a knack for knowing when to be quiet and stay away from her parent's problems. Dylan then shifts his focus back to Hannah and asks, "So are you coming with us tomorrow and if so, are you bringing a date along?" Dylan was really trying to get a rise out of her. She was trying to think of a witty response, but all she could think of was her brief attempt with Techy Ted-Drunkenly coming onto him at his computer shop, as his desk chair squeaked aloud as she pounced on top of him and the big grin on his face. She only hoped he didn't record it, with all that tech stuff about the place. She had tried to rekindle her youth with the limited options Halifax had to offer, but it didn't last long, in fact, it didn't even happen.

Dylan clicks his fingers in front of her face. "Where have you gone?" Hannah's daydreaming again. She responds with a sharp, "I'm off to the land of none-of-your-fucking-business, okay?" Dylan was taken aback, she doesn't normally swear. Eva appears at the bottom of the stairs, dressed like a vampire bride. She rolls her eyes and walks to the front door. Alex, their dog, can be heard thumping down the stairs. She stops at the bottom, notices Eva is leaving and heads back up to Eva's room to see what goodies she can find. Hannah calls after Eva, "See you later," and Eva smirks at her. "And you can log out of the CCTV 'cos I'll be changing the code," she says to Dylan. He huffs and simply replies, "Do you want a lift or not?" Hannah shakes her head. Eva who had been waiting at the door, senses the tension and couldn't pass at the chance to make a witty remark, "A woman of few words, my mother."

Hannah, a little worried and not liking her daughter's words, asks, "What's that supposed to mean?" Eva shrugs at her. Why does she feel everyone's out to get her? As he leaves, Dylan can't resist another glance at Hannah, hoping she hasn't noticed, but she did. The look lasts longer than he wanted, but he can't help but want her. Then, opening the door, he leaves with Eva. Hannah's alone, the room swallowing her whole and allowing her mind to overthink again. But this time it's begging for wine and who is she to argue with it?

Chapter Two

THE SHIBDEN INN

The taxi driver swings around the tight corner into the Shibden Inn car park as if he's an F1 driver. A bit too fast for Dylan's liking. The parking area is quite narrow and has a slight incline given the inn is situated at the valley bottom. If he was going any faster, they surely would've been in the Red Beck. The taxi driver takes no notice of Dylan's reaction and says, "Five pounds, mate, not like those London prices up here." Dylan takes out his brown leather initialled wallet, which is full of crisp new £50 notes, and hands him a tenner. "Keep the change, pal," he says as he encourages Eva out of the car as she's been glued to her phone the entire ride.

The Shibden Inn is like a forgotten piece of history. It feels like time has stood still and if you close your eyes for just a second, you could be back in the 1800s. Tucked away in the peaceful setting in the valley belly surrounded by nature trails and drystone walls, its white-painted brickwork and Yorkshire stone garden, with its beautiful blooming flowers, makes it the heart of the community. A jewel so tranquil, you could forget you are in Halifax.

The garden area is already full of visitors enjoying drinks on the quaint old benches nestled into the building front. Dylan hunches down to get through the doorways, which are all too small and low for him. The sign above the door says, 'Mind your head', but he's been caught out far too many times and has the bumps to show for it. Martha Burnside is sitting in her favourite spot, a corner seat slightly away from the rest of the room. From here she can keep an eye on everyone and see everything - the perfect place for a control freak. Her grey hair is untamed, and she has a fox-like glare, watching people come and go. She places her hand on her walking stick, notices Eva still on her phone next to the open fire and shouts to the duty manager, Preston, to bring drinks for her baby cubs and today's menu. He politely smiles and signals to a young girl to take the menu to the table.

"Oh, it's Granny's beautiful Eva," Martha gives her big sloppy granny kiss and starts messing with her granddaughter's hair, "It's a bit dry on the ends, isn't it? I'm sure some rice water will make it look better! Don't worry about the colouring, I'll get you booked in with Oliver at Sally's Salon tomorrow morning before the funeral."

Eva protests, "But Gran, it's a funeral, we don't need to dress up that fancy! Plus, it's not like he's been able to tame your wig." Martha stands firm. "Maggie deserves the best send off. She was my right-hand woman for years, and we must show her the respect she deserves. Besides, Ollie will greet us with champagne to start the day, he's very indulging is that man." Dylan interjects,

"She gets it, Mum," and he and Eva share a knowing look.

"It's alright Gran, you can keep Oliver all to yourself." Eva chuckles, knowing her ran has a soft spot for him and that he's useless with hair.

The young girl arrives at the table looking nervous around Martha and places the menus before them. "Today's special is steak and blue cheese pie. Would you like another drink?" she asks nervously.

"I'll have a pint of Vocation ale and that one will have water," Dylan says, pointing to Eva. "No, that won't do," Martha disagrees. "I've been looking over the wine list and you don't have my favourite by the glass."

The girl is stuck for words, as Martha terrifies her; she rushes to speak to the manager, hoping he will take over and she doesn't need to go back.

Soon, Preston arrives, being friendly yet firm with Martha. "Mrs Burnside," he says clearing his throat, "as you know, we don't do it by the glass." Martha giggled, replying,

"You can't judge a girl for trying." Preston grins at this, feeling he has won the battle with her, "I'll get you one of my finest to match your meal," he replies with a slight flirtatiousness in his voice. After he takes their order, he then goes off to choose from his vast wine selection, knowing that Martha has a lack of taste, and his cellar is wasted on her.

Martha leans in close to Dylan and says in a hushed voice, "They were already gossiping about you and Hannah when I came into the bar." Dylan simply replies, "They love to gossip, so let them." Martha's tone is a lot sharper now.

"You're not together anymore, and we don't have to put up with that tacky sex shop sticking out like a sore thumb in the middle of Halifax." Dylan glances around the bar, catching the eyes of the regulars who stare at him. "That thing Ruth should have left a long time ago instead of lingering around like a spare part," Martha remarks.

The young girl interrupts, puts their meals on the table, then swiftly leaves. "Mum, Ruth is a friend of mine and Hannah's from University. She's a bit eccentric, and in fact, quite mad, but to be honest, she kind of reminds me a lot of you," Dylan says, chuckling.

"No chance!" Martha cries out, her cheeks turning bright red. Eva who's busy munching on her bread, pretending to ignore the conversation, knew it's always best to avoid eye contact with Granny.

M artha tries to shift the conversation and focus her attention on Eva. After finishing her child portion of chicken and wiping her mouth with a napkin, she touches Eva's hand and says, "I've noticed you have been here a lot lately. So, what's happening with University? Is it a

boy or are you just as half-hearted as your Dad here?" She looks sternly at Dylan. "Oh, please tell me you're not gay. You've been near that Ruth for far too long." Martha's remark can be heard all around the pub, and the locals begin whispering. Eva stops for a moment and absorbs what had just been said. Why is her Gran allowed to say such things? She turns to her Dad. "Are you just going just sit there and let her talk to me like that? She's not right in the head." Dylan finds himself speechless, knowing that no matter what he says, someone would be upset.

Before he could answer, Martha waffles on. "Oh, you're just as stubborn as your mother, I see. If you are, then so be it. I mean, I experimented at grammar school." Eva shudders at the thought of her Gran's past behaviour and, having heard enough of her verbal diarrhoea, decides to fight back. "It seems like this funeral and all this death stuff has really taken its toll on you, Gran. Because I wouldn't like to believe the words coming out of your mouth are not what you really believe. Because if they are, you need correcting." Annoyed by her granddaughter's words, Martha stabs her knife into the chicken bone and pushes it aside. "Shall we order dessert? I do love a sticky toffee pudding," she says, pretending as if the conversation hadn't just happened.

Dylan heads for the toilet to give his ears a break. A few of his old school mates at the bar grab his attention. "You alright mate? Not seen you in ages. Fancy a quick pint, Dyl?" asks Dave.

"No, mate, gonna help my ma sort out Maggie's funeral," he replies. Joe Hawkins not taking the hint says, "Has Richard arrived back yet?"

"Nope."

"Who would ignore their Mum's funeral?" Dave says.

"It takes all sorts." Dylan replies, his head is banging already, so he says bye and heads straight to the gents.

Dangerous Dug, a local big mouth, was at the bar, beer in hand, trying to get Martha's attention, but she was ignoring him as usual. He hates being ignored, so starts talking out loud, to himself, "Now then, look it's the Burnsides," loud enough to get anyone's attention. As Dylan walks back to the table, Dangerous shouts, "Burnside, your ex looks stunning - she's still got it! Free to a good home now, then?" Dylan spun around to grab him, but Martha who had gotten up to use the toilet, quickly steps in between them, even with a stick she's faster than lightning. "Dug," she says firmly, "we're all in mourning for poor Maggie. Have a drink on me will you and keep it down, people are trying to enjoy themselves." Dug backtracked,

"Oh, yeah, Maggie was one of the best. Her son's a dick, mind you, but I liked her. Can I talk to you about a business venture when you've got a few minutes?" Martha, not wanting anything to do with him, replies, "I'm not conducting business, not tonight. Email my assistant tomorrow." With that, she ushers Dylan away before he did some damage.

Dylan's furious and upset with his Mum for stepping in and shouts, "Why would you buy that perv a drink?" He doesn't understand her logic. "Because, dear sweet son, he may be a cringy little creep, but Burnsides don't stoop to his level." Dylan, amazed by Martha's performance tonight, shakes his head and walks outside, pushing the door in his temper and nearly forgetting to duck. Martha then commands Eva to go with her Dad out of the building as she had to make arrangements for the following day. Eva, only too happy to escape her Gran's clutches, admits defeat and chases after her Dad.

As Eva wanders out, two dogs belonging to a farmer ran up to her. "You using that dog whisper power again?". Farmer boy Ed, whom she had always fancied from school, walks towards her. Eva

bends down and gives Scooby and Shaggy some much deserved belly rubs.

"Lambing season is soon if you wanna help out?" Ed bent down next to her. He wasn't expecting to see her. "Is that you trying to flirt with me?" Eva playfully says.

"Might be." Ed then walks into the pub winking at Eva.

"Oi, lovebirds," Dylan yells, "The taxi is here," as he puts out a cig in the plant pot. "What about Gran?" Eva asks.

"She's in her element." Dylan looks at his Mum through the window ordering poor Preston about. Poor bloke, but rather him than Dylan. With that, the two of them hop into the taxi and leave Martha to her devices.

Chapter Three

ON TOP OF THE TOWN

Hannah answered the calling of the wine and joins Ruth, her bestie, for a girl's night. But Ruth, being Ruth, wants a night out on the town and that's exactly what she's done as they are currently sitting on top of Beacon Hill looking over Halifax with a wine hamper and some crisps. "Let me see those expensive smiley white gnashers of yours," Ruth demands as she squeezes both of Hannah's cheeks tightly, trying to force a smile out of her. "You're hurting me," protests Hannah, batting her away with her hands as she tries to wriggle free.

Ruth lets go and jumps to her feet. Her shoes are off as she likes to feel the grass under her feet. She runs up and down the hillside shouting: 'Freedom' while drinking her favourite bottle of Pino. Hannah looks on. She can always count on Ruth for entertainment. "Whose freedom?" she shouts back to her and laughs at her while nearly rolling down the hill herself. It's so steep at the top of the hill, one could be forgiven for thinking Halifax is built on a mountain. "Yours, of course. Mine is as continuous as Braveheart itself," Ruth says, throwing her arms up in the air with the bottle still in hand whilst enjoying the cold evening wind hitting her face.

"Oh, is that because you're Scottish and you're brave?" Shouts Hannah. Ruth laughs and dances about. "Fuck no! I just like the movie." She blows on the top of her bottle to make a tune, but clangs her teeth on it, nearly biting her lip. "Come on, Han, you've been doing so well and then one look from that cheating wee dickhead, and you go back into your shell like a wounded animal." She pretends to die like a wounded animal and then tries to climb back up the grassy bank but keeps sliding back down.

Ruth finally made it back up and pushes the Pino bottle in front of Hannah's face. Swaying back and forth, she looks her dead in the eye. "Men, Hannah, like Dylan, get what they want all their lives. Nobody says no, so they think they can treat women..." she falls over slightly and tries not to slur her words. "And more precisely, women like us, like shit." Her knees hit the ground heavy into the mud, and she slightly squirms in pain. "And my answer to that is no!" She suddenly forgets what she's saying and lays back on the grass hugging her empty bottle like a baby.

Hannah picks at the grass around her, trying to hold back her emotions. "He was always good to me up until that fucking Claire girl. Sometimes I wish I hadn't opened that envelope and seen those pictures, the two of them together. Laid naked the same way he used to cuddle me," she cries.

"Nooo!" Shouts Ruth Loudly and jumps up, putting her finger to Hannah's mouth. "You had blinkers on and that one vanilla shit coloured envelope. Why are they even that shit colour?" Ruth ponders to herself, then falls again into Hannah's face. "It gave you your power back and opened your eyeballs." She tries to pry open Hannah's eyelids but Hannah hits her away. "My power?" asks Hannah, trying not to laugh at Ruth's attempt at a pep talk.

"Yes, the power of grey skull," Ruth says, and launches at her, pretending to wave a sword in the air. "Like Shera." Ruth starts battling the air with her pretend sword. "You are a bloody nutter, but I love you." Ruth's about to fall over again, but Hannah reaches out, grabbing her before she does.

Ruth, now in full flow, gives an encouraging, yet slightly drunken, speech: "Seriously Han, you're in charge of your own destiny now. No one else can give you what you need - only you and me, of course, as your best friend," she adds with a smug grin.

"Oh, Mystic Ruth - my favourite friend," Hannah says with a laugh.

The air cools and the scent of burning logs wafts in from the distance. Looking over the skyline of Halifax, a few rays of sunlight peek through the clouds, illuminating the Piece Hall - it looks like a Roman marble structure, sparkling in the faint light. Remembering how Ruth used to love Dylan as much as she did back at University, Hannah was hoping to reminisce over the old days, but Ruth wasn't having any of it and quickly downplayed the question of loving Dylan. Yes, she did love him back then but their relationship was more like siblings than a lover and it's hurting her to see her friends break up, but she's still in shock about what he did.

Hannah has always been there for Ruth. Since the moment they met she knew this person saw her heart. With that, Hannah was the first-person Ruth ever came out to. She didn't question her or disapprove. She simply just already knew. She always had her back, even when Ruth's mother struggled to understand who she was, and Ruth didn't have much of a clue either. Unsure of her own feelings, Hannah was her guiding light; so no, she won't let her past friendship with Dylan get in her head. The focus is to bring back the old Hannah and help her realize the person she is and has always been.

Ruth pulled the picnic blanket up off the grass and over them both, snuggling her head into Hannah's neck. "Best pals," she says. "You, me, and Dylan have a long history. That's true. But right now, he has hurt you and I won't let that stand." She kissed Hannah softly on the cheek and for that moment Ruth smiles and is in her happy place.

"You've got me and Eva. It might not be easy at times, but we're like the Pyramids - small when you look at them from afar, but when you start to dig you realise how deeply embedded they are in the ground. Solid and long-lasting." Hannah burst out laughing.

"What on earth have you been reading, or should I say watching on tv? That was deep!" Ruth smiles drunkenly.

"Yeah, that's me - deep like the river Clyde," and takes another swig from the bottle. Hannah grabs the bottle and looks at Ruth. She had been wanting to ask her some questions, but knew Ruth was never very open about her relationships - tough on the outside, but private on the inside.

She takes a moment and quietly asks, "Have you heard from Zofia lately? I know you liked her." Ruth says nothing and stays silent, avoiding making eye contact and pretends she's sleeping. Hannah knew she shouldn't push too hard, but she was curious to find out what was bothering her. Ruth opens her eyes wide and sits up. "We do message each other occasionally." She looks to the ground and pokes her finger into the mud, lost in her thoughts. Hannah was surprised, as Ruth usually gives nothing. However, seeing Ruth looking lost, she decides not to push her any further and let it drop.

"Are you still all right for the funeral tomorrow?" Hannah doesn't want to go by herself. "Definitely," Ruth perks up and responds with enthusiasm. "Free food at the Shibden, always down for some tasty grub." Hannah pushes her over playfully.

"You dick!" Hannah laughs at her, always up for a freebie, our Ruth. She just wishes Maggie had been able to recognize Richard for what he was, disappearing like that and not even saying goodbye to his own Mum. What kind of son can live with that?

16

Now Ruth was more interested in the conversation, she leans back on her elbows. "Can you imagine Richard taking some of Moaning Martha's money with him?" she snickers.

"Don't!" Hannah says, "I feel bad."

"Why?" Ruth asks. "They pushed you out and trusted that idiot. They got what they deserved." Ruth states indignantly.

"Yeah, but Maggie was the best," Hannah says. "And she deserved better."

"Well," Ruth continues, "we all deserve better."

Ruth suddenly becomes distracted by a dog walker and turns to Hannah. "Have you noticed that guy in the hoodie walking by? He's been back and forth a few times." Hannah looks around but doesn't see anyone. "Not noticed." Hannah had in fact noticed him but didn't want Ruth making a scene. There were a lot of strange people about and except from the regular taxi driver that was soon to turn up they were pretty much alone. So, no need to provoke anyone.

Ruth steadies herself, stands up and shouts, "Get up!"

"You can hardly stand still on your own," Hannah laughs.

"Right, then," Ruth holds up her bottle and motions for Hannah to do the same. "Here's to Maggie, a diamond in the heart of the valley, dearly missed but never forgotten. And to Hannah - may she realise how incredible she is and does not need a man to confirm this. May she find a new path in the world with a love that is equal." The girls then burst out laughing and fall back onto the grass.

After a few moments, Ruth stops laughing as her vision becomes hazy. She feels nauseous, and then projectile vomits on the grass over Hannah's blanket. Hannah, expecting nothing less, says, "Well, that was definitely a night to remember. Let me help you so you can sleep it off. "The taxi is already waiting at the bottom of the hill." With legs like jelly, Ruth says, "Just roll me down," whilst waving her hands about in an attempt to not fall over. "Come on, lightweight," Hannah says, tucking her arm in hers.

Just then, they hear a voice calling them from the bottom of the hill. It's Arjan, who's waiting to pick them up. He was worried as the signal on his phone was weak and so walked along the path to make sure they're okay. "Do you need assistance, Ms Burnside?" he asks.

"No," Hannah shouts. "It's Hannah always, just Hannah." She helps Ruth into the taxi. "Sorry," Ruth mumbles before leaning over and passing out on Hannah's lap.

"Good night then?" Arjan enquires, looking down at Ruth. He is getting used to this, Hannah has used his Uber service for a while, and they have become quite friendly. Hannah looks at Ruth, who was snoring. "For her, yes; for me, probably not," she responds.

"Oh," Arjan says. "Perhaps some music to clear your head on the ride home?" Hannah smiles.

"Please try to take the easiest route. We don't want to decorate your back seat tonight."

Chapter Four

LITTLE RED LINES

Eva's room is in complete darkness, just the way she likes it. Hearing footsteps creeping about, she wakes and slowly opens one sleepy eye, watching her Mum pull back the purple curtains. The morning sun illuminates her room like a bonfire, and she quickly throws the duvet over her head, turns onto her side, and wipes the saliva from the side of her face with her pyjama sleeve. There's no way in hell she is getting up yet, as her alarm hasn't even gone off. "Come on Baby Sloth."

Hannah bends down and lovingly rubs Eva's hair. "You're gonna be late! I've already called you three times. Your Dad is going to be here in five minutes to pick you up for the funeral car." Hannah looks about the room and starts picking up socks from the floor which Eva has kicked off during the night. *Why does she still wear socks to bed? Even though it is kind of cute*, she thinks. Not quite listening to her Mum, Eva then sits bolt up in bed. "What do you mean he'll be here in five? My alarm hasn't even gone off yet." Eva throws off the duvet and rummages around on the floor for her mobile. "Shit!" she shouts.

"Watch your language," Hannah says.

Eva gave her a knowing look, like she can talk lately.

"I thought I had pressed it last night, but I must have been distracted by the earthquake of snoring coming from the spare room," she says while scrolling through her social feeds.

Snoring, what snoring? Hannah looks at the dog on the floor who's not yet moved an inch. *Oh yeah,* Hannah thinks. Ruth had had a few drinks, but at least she had made it to the toilet instead of decorating the taxi this time. She must have sneaked out early without waking them up, but it's not like her to do that. Normally, Ruth would wake her up or jump into bed for a chat. How odd.

Hannah sits on the edge of the bed playing with the dirty socks. "How was the family meal?" she asks, pretending she doesn't really care but she couldn't help but feel a little left out. It's still strange not being part of everything. "Fine," says Eva, and although she's dying to tell her Mum about Gran's comments, she doesn't want to be stuck in the middle of the separation. Sometimes it feels like there is no way out between her parents. Noticing that her Mum looks a little put out, she says, "Gran seems pretty upset about Maggie; you know she is paying for everything," and continues to put her trackie bottoms on.

"How kind," Hannah answers sarcastically.

"Don't be like that Mum." Eva's annoyed at her now.

"Okay," says Hannah, "I will play nice today for your sake, not mine." Eva just ignores her and picks up her phone.

K nowing that Eva's annoyed, she grabs her pillow and starts playfully hitting Eva with it. Eva tries hard not to retaliate, puts her hands on her face and says, "Mum, stop it I'm not five," but not one to walk away from a good old pillow fight, she starts tickling her Mum. Hannah laughs and chases her to the bathroom. Eva locks the door, laughing at her. "Okay, you've got two mins to shower and then straight downstairs." Hannah walks to the bedroom door, and looks around the room at the mess *Oh, to be so carefree,* she thinks to herself as she eyes Eva's clothes and make up all over the room and Alex the dog happily lying in the middle of it all.

She grabs a few items for the wash and heads downstairs, but as she gets to the bottom, she's taken aback to find Dylan casually standing there waiting for her in the hallway. "You shouldn't have let yourself in," Hannah says.

"The door was wide open," he scolds. "You know you should lock it now you're living alone out here." She strides past him and adds,

"Who said I was alone?"

"Oh, I know you aren't," he replies with a hint of jealousy.

"What did you say?" Hannah snaps.

"Nothing," Dylan replies. He's not in the mood for an argument.

"She'll be five minutes," Hannah informs him, before heading to the kitchen. Dylan follows her into the kitchen and runs his hand over the granite worktop. "I've seen her talking to the farmer boy from the other side of the valley. Can't she find someone better than that?" Hannah sees red at his comment and drops the washing into the basket. "Dylan, she can choose who she wants." He bites his tongue and simply replies, "I'm going to use the toilet."

He goes to the downstairs toilet that backs onto the guest room and stops to look at his old office. It has been cleared out and filled with packages labelled: 'Pleasure Not Sin' from Ruth and Hannah's pleasure business. He is devastated that she's started to erase him bit by bit. He finishes his business in the toilet and goes to grab the towel from the shelf to dry his hands, but he pulls too many off and hears something hit the floor. He kicks it with his foot and looks down to see a white plastic stick. He picks it up and his eyes widen when he realises what it is. His mind goes back to four weeks ago when he and Hannah had sex on the coffee table after he came to get his things and found her crying on the sofa. After the deed she then made him leave and said it was their last goodbye.

As much as he doesn't want to admit it, he misses her, misses being so close to her warm, soft perfumed skin that makes him crave her more. That night they shared was electric, just to be intertwined with her, but he left early to make it back to London. That weekend he'd been devastated because he understood that the moment they had shared, that wonderful pleasure, was the concluding chapter of their marriage.

He glances back down at what is in his hands and sways when the realisation of what the two bright red lines meant on the small plastic stick. A positive pregnancy test! Overcome with shock he stands there, gawping at his reflection in the mirror - what was he going to do? Not expecting this, he takes a long, hard look at himself, thinking it was the last thing he expected to find today. Perhaps having another baby could help heal their broken relationship, and she may even forgive him.

It's possible. Given that she had sex with him, she must feel the same way, or she wouldn't have done that. He loves her with all his heart and has never given up hope that perhaps she could forgive him. Could this be the answer? He put the test in his pocket and heads for the kitchen. Should he say something now or wait a few days, make some plans, and show up with flowers?

Heading towards Hannah and having a tight grip on the stick in his pocket, Dylan reaches out to touch her but is surprised to see Eva. "Dad, you look dog rough." She's standing at the bottom of the stairs, eating dry toast. "Yeah, probably had a few too many last night," he responds, still taken aback by his discovery. "Well, that seems to be a common consensus around the valley this morning," Eva notes as she looks at her mother. Hannah simply grins. Dylan can't take his eyes off his wife, and Hannah notices this and feels uncomfortable, so tries to change the topic.

"So, you'll go with Dad in the car, and I'll collect Ruth and meet you all at the church." She starts to be quite authoritative, wanting Dylan to leave the house. Dylan steps back, still gazing at Hannah. He seems a bit confused. Eva, who's watching him comments, "It should be an interesting day." She then gives her toast to the dog, grabs her coat, and goes out to the car.

Dylan's still standing there just watching and wanting her. Hannah can't deal with anymore of the staring asks him, "Do you have something to say?" He wants to say so much, he would do anything for a second chance, but the look on her face told him it wasn't going to happen. He hardens his grip on the pregnancy test and replies softly, "No, see you at the church." Hannah notices the tears in his eyes, and seeing the sadness, she slowly approaches him, her expression gentle as he appears vulnerable. They share a moment, but it's broken by Eva honking the car horn. Dylan quietly pulls himself together and whispers, "See you soon."

He pauses by the front door, hesitant at first, but then says as he stares out at Eva, "All I ever wanted in the world was you, me, and Eva. I broke that, no excuse, it was all down to me. And for that Hannah, I am truly sorry." He then steps out of the door and closes it firmly behind him.

Chapter Five

SOUTH SIDE OF THE VALLEY

Reverend Adio Brown and his wife Leanne are standing under the wooden arch entrance of the church, comforting Martha as they welcome people for Maggie's service. Martha wipes away her tears from under her glasses and whispers to the reverend about how she and her late friend Maggie used to visit the church when they were young, walking up the hill and down into the valley below, without phones or any other distractions in the good old days. A faint smile appears on Martha's face as she fondly remembered their times together.

The church, made of old stone, stands proudly at the top of the valley with a view of Shibden Park from its peak. Even though the church is small, it's still an integral part of the town. Maggie attended every Sunday, and her son Richard was christened there. Reverend Brown always had time for Maggie and tried his best to steer Richard on a, let's say, sinless path. One that Richard decided not to take.

Pushing Leanne out of the way, Martha takes the Reverend's arm. "I may have moved away from this side of the valley, but a girl never forgets her roots." Leanne, who's a strong woman and not one to be messed with, then interrupts, "The hearse has arrived; let me help you to your seat Mrs Burnside." She takes Martha's hands off her husband and with a firm grip, she then guides Martha to the forefront, beside

Dylan and Eva. Leanne then sits on the seat next to Adio glaring at Martha. No other woman shall mark her man.

Ruth and Hannah sit five rows back. Dylan glances at Hannah, who had her head down, reading the order of service. He thought to himself that she looked good, given the circumstances. He notices Ruth scowling at him. *Damn, now she looks terrible*, he thinks.

"He's giving you some odd looks." Ruth elbows Hannah in the ribs.

"I don't care," Hannah replies under her breath. Hannah notices that Richard hasn't made an appearance. "Not even shown up for the funeral," she whispers.

"Good, because I'd have no problem sticking this vape in his eye." Ruth does a stabbing motion.

The organist stretches his fingers before he starts to play, and as the cedar-wood coffin makes its way down the stone-floor aisle, everyone rose to their feet. White roses are strewn across the top, and Hannah can't stop her tears. Noticing this, Ruth hands her a tissue and Hannah inspects it. "How long have you kept this in your pocket?" Ruth snatches it back off her. Reverend Brown addresses the packed congregation that overflowed with friends and mourners that spilled outside into the gardens. Maggie may not have had close family, but she had the love of the whole community, supporting many charities. Whenever a raffle needed tickets sold, Maggie was always the first one to step up.

Once everyone was sitting down and the Reverend had finished his opening words, Martha makes her way to the pew. As her cane echoes through the church, everyone stays silent, as if they were waiting on Churchill's speech. Martha clears her throat and leans heavily on the pew to support herself. "So many of you have come here today to pay tribute to our dearly departed Maggie Lockwood. Unfortunately, someone who mattered to her the most is not present today." There was a collective gasp as the congregation waited to hear what Martha had to say next. "Her only son, Richard M Lockwood, has asked me to say a few words on his behalf."

Hannah and Ruth exchange glances of amazement. Richard had been missing for eight months, having stolen money from Burnside Holdings, and was thought to have left the country. Martha takes a moment, notices that all eyes are on her and then makes a statement nobody was expecting. "You are all aware of the issues we had concerning business matters. This is now resolved, and that he is now free to do as he wishes." Dylan looks on. He was unaware of this decision. Typical for Mum to pull the rug from under him. She then reads his note aloud:

"Dear Mum,

May you rest in peace knowing I love you and we will meet again someday. You, me, and the cats. Love Ricky, your boy."

Martha looks unsteady, and Eva and Dylan go up to the pew to give her support. She clears her throat and continues her speech. "On behalf of myself and my family," she says, looking at Dylan. "We loved Maggie like she was our own and a big part of us is now missing. Maggie, know that you are eternally loved, my dear friend, I will mourn you more than you will ever know." A loud bang is heard as the church door slams; Martha looks but can't see who just left. She then blows a kiss towards the coffin and makes her way back to her seat.

Ruth leaves the church before Hannah to get some fresh air and notices a car speed off but is too unwell to care much. Inside, Hannah tries to avoid Martha on her way out, as it's the part where you had to shake hands and say your goodbyes. But she wasn't fast enough. Martha stands in front of her and gives her a long look. "I know Maggie had a great fondness for you and she would be glad to know you came to say goodbye," Martha says. Hannah, still in shock over the speech, replies, "That was quite a surprise. When did you get the message from Richard? How kind of you to be so forgiving of his wrongdoings." Martha responds calmly, "I am a very forgiving person, and given the circumstances, Maggie would have wanted it that way. Oh, and I wouldn't have missed the money either. Not like I need it." With that, Martha spun around and hobbles out of the church.

"Bitch," Hannah mumbles under her breath. "Just look at her, the wicked witch of West Yorkshire - all polite, caring community member on the outside, but rotten to the core on the inside and in time it will be exposed." Hannah couldn't help but wish she could knock that stick from her hands and watch her struggle. *Oh God.* Ruth is rubbing off on me, she thinks. Eva comes up to her, asking if she could go to The Shibden with her. Hannah gives her a hug. Glad she's chosen to be with her and not the witch. Realising they haven't seen Ruth for a while, they go looking for her so they can leave. They begin to search the surroundings before Eva remembers that she saw her at the car park earlier. The two of them make their way down the slippery, wet gravel hill to the car park and hear gut wrenching noises coming from behind their car. Ruth was bent over, throwing up on the grass.

"**I** didn't realize you had that much to drink," Hannah says softly, gently rubbing Ruth's back. Ruth wipes her mouth with her sleeve and tries to stand up. "Oh, classy Ruth," Eva says.

"Can we just go, please?" Ruth asks, getting into the backseat of the car. "I need to lay down for a bit," she says closing her eyes and putting her hat over her face. As Hannah and Eva get into the car, Dylan approaches. Hannah opens the window, and he leans in. "Another wild night, Ruth?" he asks.

"Go away!" Ruth grumbles, turning away from him. He laughs at this as he enjoys annoying her. He then turns to Eva.

"You not coming with us?"

"I'd rather stick pins in my eyes," she snaps.

He steps back from the window, adjusts the collar of his wool coat, and then walks away hurt over her stinging words. Hannah winds the window up and they set off.

"Eva, you really shouldn't speak to people like that. That's not how we brought you up." Hannah sighs, keeping her gaze on the road. Eva simply shrugs and leans against the window, her hot breath fogging up the glass. As they drive past Ed, he winks at Eva, causing Hannah to chuckle and Eva to blush. They pull to a stop so Ed's sheep could cross the road. "Do you think he was waiting for you before letting the sheep cross? Maybe you two should take a roll in the hay." Hannah teases. From the dry-stone wall, Ed gives Eva puppy dog eyes, but she pretends to look at her phone. Hannah shouts from the window, "Ed, if you're interested, we've got free drinks at Shibden in five minutes, courtesy of Captain Martha Burnside." He nods, hops off the wall and shuts the gate to the field.

"Have you finished embarrassing me now?" says Eva, looking up from her phone. Hannah smirks and replies, "No, darling. I'm just getting started. That's my job as your mother." A whiny voice from the back seat pipes up, "Hey, Chuckle Brothers, can we get to the pub? I'm starving!" Ruth sits like a zombie, declaring, "I've got the munchies!" and burps in Eva's ear. "Mum, she's minging!" Eva screams. Ruth laughs.

"You should've gone with 'Daddy Big Bucks' if you didn't want to hang out with these hot dogs." Eva shakes her head in despair. Why is her family so odd? "What are you talking about? Ruth, you're weirder than Mum."

"I'll take that," Ruth smiles and punches the roof of the car.

Hannah realizes Ruth needs to settle down, as she still appears to be intoxicated. As if she read Hannah's thoughts, Ruth yells out, "Drunk on life, my Yorkshire princess," and then flops back down on the back of the seat, meowing like a cat. Eva and Hannah exchange glances, evidently not surprised by this behaviour, and Hannah keeps on driving.

Chapter Six

THE SPEECH

The Shibden bar is already packed with people taking advantage of the free drinks. Donald, a local, perches on the corner bar stool, flat cap pulled over his brow growling out loud at the visiting customers. He's a proud man and refuses a free drink from the 'money grabbing Burnsides' but not too proud to grab a handful of free nuts. He opens his side pocket and Archie, his hamster, sticks his head out, takes the nut, and disappears back in.

The news that Martha has put a lot of money behind the bar spreads and Dangerous Dug is taking full advantage despite a few disgruntled employees complaining. Martha's aware of this, and as always, she enjoys the control it gives her. Throw them a little something and they all come sniffing round. She likes to keep the locals close enough to have their ear.

Staff are running around trying to make sure everyone is taken care of and begin directing them to the breakfast room that has been set up for the funeral tea. Preston is following Martha as she gives him orders. Eva has now retreated to the quiet sofa downstairs, hoping to avoid as many people as possible; a difficult task in an area where people feel like they have some kind of ownership of you because of your family name.

Dylan is standing on the upstairs balcony, taking a long draw of his cigarette as he listens to Chris Jenkins, an old grammar school friend, who was talking nonstop about her horses, obviously hoping Dylan would convince Martha to use her stables. From above, he then sees Hannah and Ruth chatting in the car park and watches them. He stops paying attention to Chris now as his mind becomes distracted by the pregnancy test.

His phone rang, rang off again and then kept ringing. He pulls it out of his pocket and saw that he had ten missed calls from Claire, Richard's ex-assistant, and the woman he'd had a one-nighter with that ended his marriage to Hannah. He wished she would get the hint and leave him alone, but she was persistent and had been calling him every day for the last two weeks, saying she needed to talk to him face to face. The last thing he wants to do is face her. She is the epitome of his of his flaws.

Preston walks over to Dylan, trying to avoid Martha by mingling with the crowd. He asks if Dylan wants another drink, but Dylan says he's about to go downstairs to the bar when he sees Hannah walk through the entrance. He knew this was his moment to catch her and address what he's found. He hoped it could be a game changer for them. He apologises to Chris for interrupting her, takes her hands tightly and assures her he will speak to Martha. Ever so grateful, Chris promises to bake him a cherry pie and rubs his hand suggestively. She whispers, "My pies are always warm and moist for you, Dylan." Dylan on the other hand can't wait to get away from her. Her pie is one he doesn't want to touch.

Ruth walks in through the side door and bumps into him. He wasn't ready to be confronted by her yet. Knowing the Ruth from his Uni days, he knew what he was about to face. He tries to talk to her, but she cuts him off. She doesn't want to hear his excuses or anything else that comes out of his lying fucking gob. She's chosen a side and she is sticking to it. He broke something more than his marriage and to Ruth that can't be taken back. "You are nothing to me" were her last words to him before she left him standing there speechless, ashamed of his actions.

The bar staff look at him. "I think you could use a drink, mate," Andy with the two Poodles at the adjacent table remarks. Dylan goes to answer back but notices Andy's drinking companion is a large Carp fish, and he's taking selfies with it. Dylan decides that is one situation he doesn't want to be involved in today. He requests a double whiskey, gulps it down, slams the glass on the bar and steps outside.

Hannah, who had been at the other side of the bar, witnesses the entire incident and although a part of her found delight in Ruth putting him in his place, she still wants to go out and console him. However, old habits die hard and that wasn't her responsibility anymore. She notices Andy's fish, and baffled, decides not to approach either. Spotting Eva hiding from the world on the sofa, she convinces her to join them upstairs, though Eva gave a strong case against suffering her Gran's company again after the meal last night. Hannah was having none of it. As much as she herself did not want to be here, Maggie would have wanted them to be together at a time like this.

Eva sees Ed grab a beer and then approach Andy and his fish. She suddenly gets nervous at the sight of him, and she doesn't know why, so she counts to five and then walks over and pats Andy's fish as she follows her Mum upstairs. She stands at the other side of the room, keeping her distance from him but also keeping an eye on him. She was once friends with him, well, in junior school anyway, but she didn't see him much when she went to Grammar. He always seemed like the local bad boy that everyone wanted to hang with. Back then she hated the sight of him because he was always winding her up and calling her stupid names like 'Goth Girl' or 'Posh Knocks'. Lately she keeps bumping into him, and she feels strange to be attracted to 'Farmer Boy'.

Ed notices her hovering at the back and calls out, "Hey, Goth Girl!" It irritates her instantly. Why is he so annoying, but at the same time why is she so attracted to him? It was infuriating for her. Yes, she had been a teen goth and still was at heart. He walks towards her, and she begins to feel the hairs on her neck stand on end. Eva's heart beats faster as he gets closer. Towering over her, she looks at his clothes and trying disguise her feelings says, "You could have made an effort to get the sheep shit off you." He pokes his holey jeans and pretends to wipe himself down. He was actually trying to impress her. Could he like her too? She was sure he was all flirty last night.

"Did silly bollocks want me to make a good impression, then?" Eva rolls her eyes and Ed looks down at his pint and she's sure she seen a little blush under his freckles. "I see your Grandma is spoiling everyone with her money. But a free beer is a free beer in my book." Ed half smiles, hoping for a response, but clocks the food. "Looks like they are serving up pie but no bloody peas... and is that Yorkshire pudding with beef wrapped inside it? Come on, let's get some!" He grabs Eva's hand, and she lets him, dragging her to the buffet that had been laid out on the table. It was full of locally sourced dishes, and everyone was queuing up for their share.

Hannah scans the room for Ruth, assuming she must have gone to the toilet yet again. She stands at the back out of everyone's way, sipping her G&T - a Yorkshire Rhubarb Gin and Elderflower Tonic with some dried fruits - one of her local favourites. Once people had settled down, having attempted to clear the buffet table, Martha taps on her glass and Ruth suddenly appears next to Hannah, sipping some water.

"Wonders never cease," Hannah remarks to her, looking at the water in Ruth's hand. "Let's see if she can pull off two show stopping speeches in one day. The power must be going to her head." Ruth's eyes are wide, watching to see what comes next.

Martha surveys the gathered crowd. All eyes are on her, and she begins to speak but stops when she notices Dylan sitting next to her, looking lost in his glass of whiskey. Martha hates to see her only son in such a state, and a flicker of guilt can be seen across her face. She can't let her guard down in front of this pack of animals, so she sets her notes aside. Deciding on a new course of action. "Thank you once again for joining us here to celebrate Maggie. I raise a glass to everything that was her life." She holds up her white wine and everyone follows. She continues, "I believe life should be enjoyed to its fullest. When my husband Jock passed away ten years ago, I set out to make the most of things, even though I miss him dearly every single day."

Dylan holds her hand as she gazes down at him. He wishes his Dad was still around too. Hannah looks on and she begins to well up. Gunner was the best of the best, a true gent. He settled in these parts from Scotland with nothing and worked his entire life for his fortune. He believed in the value of people and was never a show-off. A quality Hannah always saw in Dylan in the early days of their life together.

Once Martha gauges everyone's reaction, she struggles to keep her emotions in check, dabbing her eyes before continuing. "Going forward, we should all begin anew. You are all aware of the breakdown of my son's marriage." Dylan lifts his head from his glass and he and Hannah glance at each other in disbelief. Hannah steps forward, but Ruth swiftly pulls her back. "Regardless of what has happened, the family will always love and cherish Hannah. But it is time for both parties to move on. With the divorce comes new opportunities for both; we appreciate the support you have all shown in these difficult times."

Hannah's so shocked she's trembling; nothing has been discussed or finalised. Divorce is something that seemed so distant. Did he want to get rid of her so much as to make an example of her in this manner? Is there someone else in his life now? Ruth takes Hannah's hand and quickly leads her downstairs and out of the building before it kicks off.

Ed is munching on his third Yorkshire pudding and enjoying being in the heart of the drama. He turns to Eva and says, "Your Gran's quite the character. She's got balls, I tell you that." But Eva has also disappeared. He just shrugs and searches for any desserts on offer.

Martha sits down, looking content with herself. Dylan leans in and hisses, "What the hell, Mum? We haven't discussed anything or come to any agreement!" He says angrily. Martha replies confidently,

"No, but it's for the benefit of the family that you both get a push." Dylan slams his fist on the table. "No, Mum, it's all about what's convenient for you!" He gets up and announces he's taking the first train back to London. Martha, aware that everyone is looking at her, takes a sip of her wine, raises her glass at those glaring and orders another bottle, now surer of herself than ever.

Hannah's hyperventilating heavily in the car park, walking up and down, back and forth. "What is she thinking?" she sobs.

"It's a control thing, she loves it, she's a vile snake," Ruth replies, trying to calm her before she spontaneously combusts. Hannah puts her hand to her forehead. "Where's Eva? She must have heard all that," she says. Ruth looks around the car park, sure she saw her leave the building before them. "Let's just get out of here and you can call her." Hannah hesitantly agrees. She and Ruth get into the car and sped out of the car park in search of Eva.

Eva had been standing in the top car park watching her Mum and Ruth with tears streaming down her face as they drove away. She didn't want to be near either parent right now. Ed, who had sacrificed his dessert to come find her, slowly shuffles up to her. "Please go away, Ed," she attempts to push him away, not wanting to deal with any of his smart-arse remarks. "Evy, Eva...you need a friend. Come to mine for a bit, me mam can make you the best Yorkshire brew." He rubs her arm and softly caresses her cheek before pulling her in for a hug.

Chapter Seven

VAG

Well, the dust may not have settled, but it's been a good few weeks since the drama that was 'Martha's twin speeches' at Maggie's funeral. Dylan has decided it was safer to stay down south, ignoring his Mum and giving Hannah more breathing space while he gains the courage to speak to her, if he can bring himself to, because it's easier to avoid her. The valley itself just moves along with the season, blossoming gently into spring.

People from all over the world start to arrive for Ann Lister's birthday week. Hotels are filling up, Shibden Park and the Piece Hall are buzzing with activities and shops are full of tourists as Halifax prepares for a booming trade season.

Speaking of trade, 'Pleasure Not Sin', a small shop located on the cobbled backstreets of Halifax town centre is open for business. Although it's mostly operated online, the store is mainly used to stock goods and as an office base. As Hannah walks in carrying two lattes for her and Ruth, two young lads are standing near the condom tree and freeze when they notice her. She looks around but there's no sign of Ruth. Their little visit has become a common occurrence, as teenagers often dare each other to enter the shop, despite there being nothing different at the front of the shop from what you would find online and in high street stores these days.

One boy had a packet of ten play-safe condoms, large and ribbed, in his hand while the other was sniggering. Hannah places the coffees on the table next to her - a vagina-shaped glass table she has only now noticed. Rubbing her hands together, she says, "So, boys not sure of the sizing? Do you need any help?" She gestures towards the safe sex and genital health leaflets beside them. "At least you're ready to play safe. Are they teaching you that at school?" The boys try to put the pack back quickly but end up knocking over some jelly boob packets. "Just looking," one mutters nervously, and they push past her and run out of the shop. "Don't forget, we do buy one get one free on Willy Wednesday if you're interested," she shouts after them, and then laughs as she watches them sniggering as they run down the street.

No sign of Ruth on the shop floor, not like her to leave the door unlocked if she's not about. So, Hannah locks the front door and takes the coffees upstairs, looking back at the tables as she goes. It's ugly, but she's sure Ruth thinks otherwise. On the way up the stairs, she hears the flushing of a toilet. Ruth appears looking very pale and clammy. She dabs her face with a wet towel. "I heard those wee shites, but I didn't have the energy to chase them away again today. You'd think they would be sick of it by now," she says, as she opens the coffee lid and adds extra sugar to it.

"The Vag table is a recent addition, is it?" Hannah motions towards the downstairs trying not show her disgust. "Yes," Ruth says excitedly and looks pleased with herself. "It's a find, don't you just adore it?" Ruth stirs her drink, looking ever so happy with her purchase. "I saw it on a supermodel's house show. She had this tunnel between her bedroom and bathroom," Ruth clarifies.

"And from that you purchased a vag table?" Hannah asks. Ruth is confused as to why she would ask this. It seems an obvious thing to want in a shop like this. "Yes," she agrees, as it makes perfect sense to her. "Plus, they threw in a coaster and 250 pens with venus flytrap vaginas on the top," she exclaims, clapping her hands in joy and holding out a pen for Hannah to have. "Can you imagine if that was real?" Hannah laughs along with her. "If it was, it would be a bloody mess!"

Hannah stops laughing and gets all serious as they have an important day ahead. "Do we have everything we need for this council meeting?" She gets her notes out of her bag so they can go through things before they leave. "Fucking knob cheese!" Ruth blurts out. "That's what he is. He's been against us and our pleasure business since the beginning. The only reason he's pushing his agenda now is because of that divorce speech. He thinks that since you won't be a Burnside anymore, he has free rein over us." Ruth has it in for Councillor Davis Jeremy of the Business Council. He has called them in for a meeting regarding local complaints about the business.

A Gina G song starts playing loudly. "That's my phone, I'll meet you outside." Ruth looks nervous to answer and holds the phone to her chest. She quickly goes downstairs as Hannah shouts, "The taxi is picking us up since my car is in for an MOT. Don't take ages." Hannah spots an invoice on the desk for a big order of dildos called 'Thank the D'. Amazed by the name, and puzzled by who comes up with these things, someone like Ruth probably. She wonders where they were going to keep them all as there's no room. She put the invoice back on Ruth's desk and walks downstairs to lock up the shop.

As she leaves and pulls the shutter down, she notices a man sat with his cardboard sign in the closed shop next to theirs. She goes over and sits next to him. He asks for money for a drink but when he realises it's Hannah, he smiles. She put some cash in his pot and asks, "Not seen you in a while, been anywhere nice?" Seems like a silly question, but she was hoping he had got a bed in a shelter and gotten some help. He explained that someone had stolen his stash, so he had moved to the train station for a while but had been moved on due to the tourist season. He had now found a nice new spot next to her shop. Hannah told him that he could always knock on her door or leave a message in the letter box if he ever needed anything. He nodded in response.

"Ruth! The taxi's here!" Hannah cries out. Ruth doesn't respond; she is just stood staring into the road. No longer on her phone. Hannah walks over and taps her on the shoulder. Ruth jumps and looks startled. "You okay?" Hannah asks, as Ruth looks distracted. Ruth says nothing and they get in the car. Hannah looks back at the shop as they drive off.

"How long has he been back?" Hannah inquires. Ruth responds with a sharp reply, "A few days. Think he's called John, I let him use the bathroom this morning." Hannah realises that this attitude is not about John, if that is his name, but about something else. "What's up? Your face is telling me something's wrong. You seemed in a hurry to take that call," she blurts out without thinking.

"What do you think is wrong? Another one of those arrogant males who thinks he can control my life?" Ruth says, as the taxi driver turns up the music as Ruth gives him a mean stare. "Please Ruth, try and stay calm. Let's just go in and hear what they have to say and then we can figure it out from there. If we go straight in on the attack right away, they'll win, and we're left with more problems."

Hannah attempts to calm and soothe Ruth. "It's just one thing after another," Ruth sighs as she turns and gazes out the window. Hannah was taken aback - Ruth was usually the one with the plan of action, and to see her so flustered was alarming. Arjan, the taxi driver, notices the silence in the back seat and takes the opportunity to speak as he had been wanting to ask this question for a few days. "Miss Hannah, would you mind if I gave you this invite?". He passes her a laminated gold envelope between the front seats. Hannah looks at the back and the front. "What's it for?" She was intrigued by the beautiful flower decorations and elephant symbol on the card.

"My son Harsmit and his business partners are opening a new restaurant in Bradford this weekend, one of many. And as a businesswoman, I would be honoured if you could attend - if you're not too busy, of course. You seem like a very busy lady." He seems shy about asking her, but also looks like a proud father. Hannah wasn't sure what to think but accepts the invite. She remembers him telling her how his son lost his wife a few years ago but can't remember which son.

She gracefully accepts. "Thank you, Arjan. I'm not sure of my plans yet, but I will keep it in mind." She put the invite in her folder and takes out her notes for the meeting. Glancing at Ruth, who was chewing on her vagina pen, "Ruth, please don't take that into the meeting," she pleads. Ruth gave her a sly grin in response. Hannah has a bad feeling about this.

Chapter Eight

PLEASURE MEETING

The main Business Hall is undergoing an extensive modernisation process, so for the time being the girls are sitting in a temporary building on some awful orange plastic chairs in a dark gloomy hallway near the town centre. It has sat empty for years, and let's say, needs a lot of TLC. Ruth's skin is crawling, she's in full irritation mode and complains to Hannah, "It's like we've gone back to the 1970s!" She wrinkles her nose in distaste. "Do you smell it? It's reeking in here. Look at those walls. They're full of tar and still yellow from when we used to be able to smoke inside!"

Ruth shakes her head and scratches it constantly. "Feel like I've got nits", noting that the place is swarming with flies and none of the windows seems to open. All she can think about is a nice, cold shower. "Holes in the carpet, no trip hazard tape here, and they want to reprimand *us*! Bunch of dicks," she adds, snapping photos of the floor. "I'm sure my Mum had Tupperware the same colour as these chairs!"

Ruth then gives the chair a shake, and the legs come off. "Fuck it! Why is this happening to me? I mean us?" Ruth exclaims, putting her head in her hands and then kicking the broken chair. "We've been doing well, making a profit, and then this knob comes for us." Her anger rose. The stuffy hallway wasn't helping and to make matters worse, her phone had no signal. She felt like a trapped animal. "I really need some air!" She pulls down her top and started fanning her bare chest with a pink, fluffy folder.

"He's keeping us waiting on purpose, just to get a reaction from you, Ruth." Hannah tries to quiet her down, but she was also finding it hard to cope with the heat and the annoying flies in the building. Opening the back of her top and attempting to fan the sweat from her lower back, Ruth goes off on one. "If I see him anytime soon, I'm having his sweaty balls off!" she says angrily and with intent.

"Who's sweaty balls are we talking about?" Hannah asks.

"That dickhead Dylan! If he had just kept it in his pants, these idiots wouldn't think they can mess with us." Ruth's face is growing red and blotchy from the heat. "Thanks Ruth, but don't you think I can take care of myself?" Hannah says softly. Ruth sighs and takes hold of Hannah's hand reassuring her she meant no harm; well apart from the Dylan part.

"Ladies of 'Pleasure Not Sin,'" a voice announces, trying to contain their amusement. "Councillor Jeremy and Councillor Gordon are ready to see you now." The girls get to their feet at the same time as if they're at court and adjust their damp clothing, wiping away the sweat from their bodies. Ruth takes out a body spray and spritzes herself, and Hannah tries not to choke from the fumes. They pause, looking at each other, and Hannah gently moves Ruth's damp hair out of her face and whispers, "We're going into battle, my friend, so please try and stay calm. I'll do the talking, as I feel the heat is getting to you. It's important." Ruth hesitantly nods in agreement, like a mischievous schoolgirl. Of course, her silence worries Hannah.

The councillors were seated behind a large wooden table with their backs to the open windows in the room. The tar-stained net curtain flaps slightly, but not much air was entering the room. Two chairs had been placed in front of the desk, and bottles of water and crystal glasses were set on the table. Before anyone could utter a single word, Ruth grabs a bottle of still water, opens it and drinks fast, downing it as if she had never tasted water. Councillor Gordon looks at her uncomfortably, as if she had just seen a wild animal rummaging through her bins.

She felt the urge to pee now seeing all the water being consumed. "It's a bit stuffy in this old building and the heating is stuck on high, apologies for keeping you both waiting," she says, coughing into her hands and wetting her lips with her tongue for hydration. "The building is very similar to your tactics and policies," Hannah implies. "Dated and in need of reform." Ruth stops drinking and shot a side glance at Hannah. *My girl's got fire,* she thought to herself.

Councillor Jeremy is sweating like a pig. His white shirt has large sweat patches under the arms and chest. He loosens his tie and takes a sip from his glass of water. "Now, let's get down to the business at hand," he says as he tries to take control and sound formal. He looks at Hannah, and she notices he looks hungry for her. He takes satisfaction from being able to overpower a Burnside, something he has longed for.

"We have received numerous complaints regarding the health and safety standards at your store, and it is necessary for us to investigate them," he waffles on. Councillor Gordan interjects,

"Nevertheless, these issues need to be looked into, and we're determined to work with small businesses to resolve any ongoing problems," She clears her throat and gives councillor Jeremy a disapproving look.

Ruth sees red and goes in for the kill. "This is all bull. What complaints? I want to see them now!" she demands banging the table, staring straight into Jeremy's eyes. He pushes back against his chair. They can hear his back sweat rub off the leather. "Language like that will not be tolerated in this chamber." His face was like a tomato.

"More like toilet chambers," Ruth sniffs the air. "I smell bullshit," she says, and points at Councillor Jeremy. He tries to stand up to reply, but Ruth is on her feet first. Leaning over the desk like a panther about to pounce on him, "You will not intimate me councillor, your title is undeserving. It gives you no power in my book. I see your slimy existence for what it really is. You can speak to my solicitor from now on. Oh, and she is also gay! And eats homophobic twats like you for breakfast." She then gives him the finger and storms out the room, slamming the door, which knocks the window off the latch, and bangs loudly shut.

He looks down at Hannah, who has her hands over her eyes. It's not how she wanted things to go, but Ruth has said her piece now. He points at her as if she's a child. "These are the types that get you a name for yourself and I will not allow it in Halifax!" He tries to continue, but Hannah pushes the table forward into his groin. "And what types are they, Councillor?" She stands in front of him with her arms crossed. "Go on, let the room know your prejudice! Human beings, that's what we all are. The only type that is not needed in this world is short-sighted people like you." She walks to the door and looks at Councillor Gordon. "I pity you for having to work with such an arsehole," she says and then closes the door behind her, which again causes the window to bang, and the net curtains to drop on Jeremy's head.

Ruth was standing outside waiting and leaning against the wall, tears streaming down her face. Hannah approaches her, shocked to see her in such distress. She attempts to lighten the mood. "A bit tense in there, huh?" But Ruth glares up at her with such fury.

"I have spent so much time working hard in this life to prove myself regardless of my sexual preference and fight to be heard and seen, but people like that don't want to see you, they are blinkered and want to put you in a box and try to control you in their small-minded world," she sighs heavily, her head thumping against the wall. "I won't allow my life to be controlled by hate from people like him, when it's only one person's voice shouting the loudest," she says sadly. Ruth gestures to her head, "I need some time alone, I need some peace and quiet in here, I am tired of fighting just to be ignored. It hurts up here Han, it was never really about the shop, it's power for him over people who dare to be different in his world," she adds, before walking away feeling defeated.

Chapter Nine

BRIXTON BROTHERHOOD

D ylan's sitting alone feeling sorry for himself. He checks his phone to see if Hannah has contacted him. There's not a thing from her, but plenty from Claire. Twenty missed calls, seven voicemails, and ten messages on his phone from to be exact. He plays with the phone in his flat, back in Brixton, and stares at it again as it also has a picture of Hannah and Eva as a screensaver. It only makes him feel sadder. After Hannah saw photos of him and Claire, he took off and ran away down south. Not being able to see the hurt in Hannah's eyes or deal with the judgement of the unofficial Valley jury.

Burnside Holdings has an office in South London - Brixton to be exact. Making it easy for Dylan to escape Halifax as it's just a short train ride back, in case Eva needs him. Additionally, his mother has no interest in the southern branches, because she doesn't like to travel or leave her realm for long. This gives Dylan the chance to create his own little kingdom away from her prying eyes. He can also put his own stamp on the company down South - a little different from the old school Burnside ways.

Claire's message comes through again. She was Richard's assistant in Accounts, but Dylan rarely interacted with her. Yeah, he thought she was attractive, but she seemed to have some unresolved issues. To this day, Dylan still can't comprehend why he had a one-night stand with her. Before that, she hadn't looked at him twice. In fact, she seemed besotted with Richard. While he had been known to black out when drinking, and the pressures of work meant this happened often; he had never done something like this before. How can he be held accountable if he cannot even remember it?

He stares into the mirror in front of him, noting that his hair is greying around the sides, but pleased he still has a full head of hair, just like his Dad always had. He regularly plays five-a-side, goes to the gym frequently and takes cold swims on the weekends. He looks after himself, and has had offers from women, but he always belonged to Hannah. She is all he ever wanted and could see himself with only her. To consider a life without her is still new to him and something he plans to rectify.

"Still a catch," he says, stroking his beard, but he exhales sadly, for he doesn't want to be a catch. His thoughts wander to the pregnancy test again when his phone rings. He assumes it's Claire again, but it's Anderson Matthews, his five-a-side teammate.

"Mate, I'm waiting for you at the Green Twig. No excuses," Anderson says before hanging up.

Anderson is sitting in front of the match with a beer and a bag of salt and vinegar crisps. Dylan approaches the bar. He can hardly wait to be paying over the odds for a shit pint. The extortionate prices were the downfall of London living compared to up north. Also, the ale is always flat and weird down south. It would be much better if it were from Yorkshire and had a proper head on it. "Two pints and some salted nuts, love," he asks the landlady. She gives him a nod and he goes to join Anderson who's shouting at the television.

"Mate, I tell yah. Linesman's on a backhander here! The game is rigged." Anderson is loud and small, an East London man born and bred. He likes to talk as if everyone in the room is part of the conversation. Dylan doesn't mind him as he's had his back since he's been here, and the bloke is a laugh. But the boy does like his sport. It's always a topic of conversation. There's never been a sporting occasion in this pub that Anderson has not been sitting on this chair for.

Francois, the Landlady, who is in her 50s, brings over the drinks to the table. "Little head on top of yours, just as you northerners like it. Mr Anderson said you like it that way and we aim to please." She gestures towards Anderson, who's grinning like a Cheshire Cat. Dylan already knows he's going to say something vulgar. "Sure, she wouldn't mind giving you a little head," and he nudges Dylan, winking at him. Dylan takes a sip of his pint and pretends to laugh but feels uncomfortable.

H is phone rings again and Dylan gets annoyed, turning it over so he can't see it. He takes a hand full of nuts and pretends nothing is wrong. Anderson's eyes dart towards the phone and he picks it up. "This bird's keen, ain't she? Thought you were still trying to get back with the old lady?" he looks at the name. "Can I slide into her DMs, Andersons got plenty of love to give ladies." He rubs his cock.

Dylan gets pissed off with him. "Fuckin rein it in, it's the crazy bird who I slept with that ended my marriage," he shouts.

"Mate, sorry, I meant no harm. I didn't know" Anderson puts on a sad face then thinks. "Are you still seeing her then?" he asks.

"No!" Dylan says sharply. He rubs his forehead. "She will not stop calling. Not heard from her in months and now every day there's a message, asking me to contact her. Pleading to clear the air." Anderson looks surprised, as he didn't expect Dylan to be so stressed and upset.

"Look man, I don't know the ins and outs of what's happened." Anderson's tone of voice has changed. He sees Dylan looks lost. He's serious and concerned and isn't acting up for the crowd anymore. "It's ok, let's just have beer and watch the second half. Maybe they will play better." Dylan tries to change the subject, but Anderson moves closer to him, staring directly into his eyes.

"Men need to talk more," he says. Dylan wasn't expecting those words to come out of his mouth. "You been watching too much telly, mate," Dylan replies. Anderson readjusts his chair and leans forward, and he's taking no prisoners. "Seriously, my Dad -" Anderson looks down and gets a little emotional, " - he, always seemed strong, was a "Bloke's Bloke", if you know what I mean. Anyway, one day he just didn't come home. My Mum was calling him every name under the sun." He puts his hands together. "He was found a few months later. Cause of death - inconclusive."

"Sorry mate," Dylan pats him on the back. Anderson continues, "What I am trying to say is we didn't know what happened, but if I could speak to him now, I would just let him talk, no judgment, just talk." He sits up straight. "So, mate, get it off your chest. Speak to her, see what she has to say. Clear your own mind." Dylan thinks about this for a moment. "What if I don't like what she has to say?" Anderson shakes his head.

"We don't get to be happy all the time, you just got to be able to muddle through the shit at times and come out on the other side. That's life." With this, Anderson gives Dylan a friendly slap on the arm and turns around and shouts at the ref on the television again.

Maybe the southern Agony Aunt is correct. What harm can it do to hear her out? Hannah will never know he has seen her again. The message said she was living in Kent. He can arrange to meet up and nobody in Halifax would find out. But make it clear to her, it's only to hear her out and stop the constant messages. Perhaps, seeing her would clear his head and then he can produce a plan to win Hannah back. If she is pregnant, she will need him by her side. Family is important to Hannah, and a second chance could be on the horizon.

Dylan goes outside the pub and gets his mobile out of his pocket. He gets Claire's number on the screen. He calls the number, and it goes to voicemail. I'm not leaving a bloody message he thinks to himself. He calls it again, and this time she answers. Her voice is cautious. "Hello Dylan, is that you?" she softly says. He struggles to speak. He didn't realise it would be this hard to talk to her. All the guilt rises to the surface, stopping him from speaking. "Hello, are you there?" she says again. Finally, he answers. "Yes, it's Dylan."

Chapter Ten

INDIANA HANNAH

It's a gloomy grey start to the day, heavy rain is coming down hard for the second day running. The only bonus is that it's watering the spring blooms of Halifax. Hannah has been sat in her car for about an hour outside Ruth's apartment. She eats a donut and drinks her coffee, looking at the rain. It's one of those renovated old Victorian mill buildings. So many have been converted, but this one comes with its own private pool and a parking space for each apartment. Due to the parking restrictions, Hannah has parked on the roadside and is waiting to see if she can get through the gate.

She tried the apartment buzzer several times but there's no answer. Ruth isn't answering her phone either and hasn't opened the shop today. Two days space is all Hannah can give; she's desperate to check on her and sits in the car trying to amuse herself by messing with the radio stations while watching for the gate to open. Not one station had a decent song. Feeling hot and stuffy, she rolls down the window slightly to let air in. A double rainbow appears over the mill apartments. Excited by this, she tries to take a picture but has sugar all over her hands from the donut she has been eating.

Since the council meeting, Hannah has been trying to give Ruth space, but she feels like she needs to be there for her since something feels off. Ruth doesn't seem herself, her outburst at the meeting wasn't like her. Yes, she's direct, but always in control. If Hannah has learned anything in the last few months, it's to trust her instincts. First it was with Richard, when he managed to get her job and Martha was extremely happy to push her out. Dylan seemed all too happy with this, like he never really wanted her in the company. She felt something wasn't right at the time but didn't act quickly enough. Then Dylan. She never imagined he was cheating with Claire. She had an intuition that something wasn't right with Claire herself. To be honest, she thought it might be a drug issue as she was always nervous and shaky, not that Claire was feeling edgy due to her excessive overtime she had been doing with her trusted husband. Makes perfect sense now as to why Dylan was eager for her to leave the business and for her work on her own projects from home.

Hannah starts thinking about everything that has happened and gets distracted from the mission at hand - to get to Ruth. Biting into another donut, she then sees a Smart car turn into the mill entrance and the gates opens. She quickly gets out of her car and almost gets hit by passing traffic while trying to make her way through the gate before it closes. "Yes!" she exclaims; feeling like Indiana Jones. Now she could go up to Ruth's flat in person without having to make any more phone calls and be ignored.

On the day that Ruth took Hannah to see the apartment complex when they opened the showrooms, she recalls that Ruth was filled with excitement when she first set eyes on the grand building, its entrance with its black steel beams and glass lift. She fell in love with the historical building when she discovered it was being converted five years ago. As Hannah goes up in the lift, her gaze is drawn to the tiled floor beneath her, set with a mural of the people gone by who used to work the mill's floors. It was designed by a local artist whose family once owned the mill.

The door to Ruth's apartment has a flower ring in Pride colours. She knocks and shouts, trying to get Ruth's attention. "I brought donuts, but I ate them," she jokes as she bends over and shouts under the door. Suddenly, the door opens, and Ruth appears in a t-shirt with the words 'Do or die' printed on it. She gave Hannah a quick appraisal as Hannah is bent over on all fours. Hands on hips, Ruth says, "Donuts are obviously not safe around you, are they?". With a wave, she reluctantly gives in and invites Hannah inside.

The curtains are drawn, blocking out any light from entering the apartment, and the couch is made up into a bed. There are dirty dishes on the coffee table. The kitchen island is littered with pizza boxes and the television is left playing loudly. Ruth walks over to the television and turns down the volume. Hannah takes a seat on the love chair. "It's not fun to wallow in misery when your bestie isn't around, is it?" She pretends to pout, her lips turned down in a frown.

Ruth plops herself back onto the couch and cuddles her blanket tightly, trying not to look at Hannah. "I wanted to deal with this alone," she sighs, but before Hannah could respond, Ruth shouts, "I miss my Zo, my Zofia!" her facial expression shows a mixture of relief and sadness. Not knowing what to say, Hannah begins to clean up. If she pretends she isn't listening, Ruth will talk more for attention, a bit like child. It works. "Don't bother, I don't usually talk about my love life. I'm so guarded, but I think I really love Zofia." Tears trickle down her spray tanned face, with only one of her fake eyelashes remaining. Hannah stops cleaning. "I thought she wasn't interested anymore," she says as she looks around for the other missing eyelash.

"She longed for a family, so we looked into using a donor." This was a huge revelation coming from Ruth, so Hannah felt the need to take a seat to digest it all. Ruth kept going, "It was her idea, I was uncertain. Zo can't have children, so I got tested, but I stopped attending the appointments and told her I wanted to remain single and be on my own." Hannah gazes at her friend lovingly and asks,

"But do you?"

"No," Ruth exclaims, standing up and throwing her arms in the air dramatically. "I was scared. It all felt so grown-up with me having to commit!" She sat back down, her head in her hands. "But now she's gone back to Poland, and I have no clue how to find her."

"Nonsense," Hannah says. "The internet knows all. I'm sure Ted the Techy can help us find her." Ruth doubted it was possible. "Okay, I was having a moment of curiosity when I messed about with him, and he is kind of sweet in a nerdy way. I'm an inner nerd," Hannah confirms to Ruth. But Hannah knows Techy Ted and his mates can find anything using the internet.

"Well, 'inner nerd', let's see if he is still speaking to you." Ruth gets up and puts her jeans on. "What are you doing?" Hannah looks on in disgust. "Getting dressed" Ruth is not sure what the problem is. Hannah is screwing her face up, Ruth smells like she has been decaying for a week. "Firstly, let's get you showered." Hannah orders Ruth to the bedroom and hands her a towel. "Okay but promise me you tell nobody about my meltdown." Ruth points her finger at Hannah.

"My lips are sealed." Hannah hits Ruth on the bum with the towel.

"Let's order some food and we can find Techy Ted tomorrow, it's Hannah and Ruth time now. Movie of your choice." Hannah looks around the room and starts to tidy up again, noting a selection of dildos. Nothing like sampling your own products, she thinks to herself. Ruth sticks her head around the bedroom door. "Nothing romantic, soppy, or funny. Let us go full horror frenzy," she says. Hannah, not a huge fan, but willing to give it a go for her friend, just nods. Ruth smiles back at her and peels the one fake lash off her eyelid. "You're the best, Han." She shouts from the shower. Hannah remembers the invite to the restaurant opening in Bradford from Arjan. She smiles to herself. "Yip and to cheer us up, we are off to Bradford tomorrow night for some quality food and girls-only night out."

Chapter Eleven

BRADFORD BOY

It had been too long since Ruth and Hannah had been out to a fancy event together. Ruth looks around her small one-bedroom apartment, which is now a mountain of clothes. Her wardrobe is not much bigger than the room itself, so she had to take every item out to build up her outfit for tonight. She holds up a leopard-print pair of platforms, with red soles and a wide-legged, satin pink jumpsuit she had bought in Milan. She seems pleased with her choice as leopard print is her go to, but suddenly feeling queasy, she rushes to the bathroom, head resting on the toilet seat, fed up with the constant fatigue. *Not again* she thought, reminding herself to make an appointment with the doctor because this was becoming a joke.

In the kitchen below the bedroom, Hannah is trying to open the prosecco without it exploding, as it seems a little warm, while holding her phone to her ear with Eva chatting away. "Where's my invite, Mum?" she whines. Hannah looks at her nails as she pulls the cork off the bottle. They need in-fills. This party is not really Eva's thing, but she plays along. "You want a night out with your Mummy and Ruth?" she asks in a toddler-like voice. "Well, come to think of it, I'd rather not, no doubt you will be home early carrying Ruth anyway," Eva replies. She wants to have an important conversation with her Mum but can see now is not the time. Sometimes there's no point talking to her when she's babysitting Ruth.

"Ed's sheep are about to pop," she changes the subject. "I've decided to help out when they do, I've done it before." She attempts to persuade her Mum. Hannah knows Eva has always had a soft spot for Ed, could always see it since they were kids. "Oh, helping Ed, are you?" She can't help but tease, as their little budding romance is cute. "I thought you hated the smell of sheep?" Eva can be heard grunting at her Mum.

"I was ten when I said that Mum," she concludes, making her excuses to finish the call.

"Ready," Ruth announces with a flourish, walking down the staircase as if she were in an 80s American soap opera. Hannah claps her hands in support and offers Ruth a pre-departure drink of prosecco. Ruth declines, but not wanting Hannah to know about her little episode upstairs, makes an excuse about not starting too early in the night. Of which neither of them believes to be true.

Arriving a little late at the restaurant, things are in full swing. They can't believe their eyes. The glass-fronted building is illuminated by low-lit purple lights, and a crowd has gathered out front. Petals are offered by the Hindi dancers, and Ruth dances along with them as they walk along the purple carpet that leads to the entrance. "It's like a movie premier," Hannah remarks in amazement. Inside, the ceiling is glistening with chandeliers - Ruth whispers to Hannah that it must have cost a pretty penny. Hannah is in awe of the beauty of the place. It's so modern but has a feel of another world as the frescos invite you into a forbidden destination.

Arjan, who invited them, makes his way over to greet them, looking proud of his son, and introduces her to his wife, children, and grandchildren. He shows Hannah the painting of India his daughter has lovingly painted on the walls of the restaurant and explains to them that it's a story of love and family from India to Bradford. Hannah gives him a kiss on the cheek and says, "You're a lucky man to have such a wonderful, loving family and for them to have put so much into this evening." Arjan beams and gives his wife a squeeze. He then looks at Ruth, unsure what to think of her as it's the first time he has seen her sober, but she's too busy sampling the buffet.

Ruth encourages Hannah over to try the buffet, but she politely declines. As she turns away, she walks head-first into a man in a red velvet suit jacket. His shoes are as shiny as the mirrors on the ceiling above. She meets his eyes; warm and inviting like golden desert sands. They warm her body, and she feels a little lost for words. Who is this creature?

Arjan appears next to her and introduces his son, Harsmit, the man in front of her, dressed in a dinner jacket and Gucci loafers, with those golden eyes. Harsmit's sweet honey scent mesmerizes her so much so that she can't formulate words to respond. He proffers his hand, but she's so captivated by his appearance to notice. Ruth interrupts and shakes his hand for Hannah before she finally breaks out of her trance and introduces herself. "Hi, I'm Hannah from Halifax," she says in broken mumbled words, and almost at once she's embarrassed by what she's saying. It's not a job interview. Hannah puts her head down and heads to the bathroom.

Ruth follows her to the toilet sniggering, asking her, "What's happened? Did Mr Bradford get your knickers in a twist?" Hannah blushes and admits that she wasn't expecting him to smell so good or to be blown away like that by one person's existence. Ruth spots some jasmine hand lotion in a basket, rubs it on her hands, then pops it in her bag. Hannah notices this and quickly tells her to stop it. "But they're freebies, Han. It wouldn't be here if they didn't want me to take it!" She pats her bag and adjusts her makeup in the mirror before they leave the washroom. Hannah shakes her head; she can't take her anywhere.

The two of them head back to the main restaurant, but Hannah couldn't resist looking for Harsmit. Her eyes dart all over the room, trying to catch just a glimpse. However, he was nowhere to be seen. Ruth drags Hannah to the dance floor and the girls mingle the night away with the guests and Arjan's family until their feet hurt. Hannah twirls around and looks up at the glistening chandeliers, and at this moment her troubles disappear as she just spins them out of her head. As she slows down, she can see Ruth looking a bit pale again. Ruth puts her hand on her belly, rubbing it gently. "I think I ate too much. I need some fresh air."

Hannah guides her outside and suggests taking a taxi back and that's when they see Harsmit leaning against the smoker's cabin with a cigar and a brandy in his hand, looking like a 1930s movies star entering the crowd. He brushes off his red jacket and places the cigar in the ashtray. Hannah felt like a teenager, all giddy to see him. She tries to behave like a grown woman and thanks him for the evening and comments on the beauty of the restaurant, this time without mumbling. Harsmit looks at her like she was a rare vintage find and let her ramble on. He then replies, "I didn't think much of Halifax before, but after tonight I can see it has potential." He then walks past Hannah, gently brushing her arm and says, "Get home safe, Halifax Hannah." She blushes, wondering if he's flirting with her or just enjoying the amusement of a rambling woman. Ruth quickly pulls her towards the car park. "Okay, love struck. Time to get in the taxi. You can get a poster of him for your bedroom wall."

On the drive home, Hannah can't help but think about the handsome Bradford Boy. He looks like a movie star. She has never been so captivated by someone so quickly before, feeling almost as if she was floating. Ruth rests her head on her lap and Hannah gently caresses her hair. "You need to get some more vitamins, Ruth. You've been like this for weeks," Hannah says.

"I don't think vitamins are going to help me," Ruth replies.

"What do you mean?" Hannah asks, confused.

"Nothing," Ruth murmurs, snuggling closer into her lap.

Hannah wonders if he bathes in honey - it's all she could smell. Maybe he has jars of it or keeps bees? She shakes her head, trying not to overthink it. They enter the valley, and the taxi stops at a set of lights. "We can head down to Shibden if you want to? Last orders aren't for another hour. Eva might be there, and Martha might as well. I've been trying to avoid her since the funeral," she says, looking down to find Ruth fast asleep, snoring softly. That's kind of sweet, Hannah supposes. She smiles, stroking her face.

The light turns to green, and the driver accelerates, turning onto the narrow, cobblestone road that leads up to Burnside Cottage, where Hannah lives. The valley is silent and still; all that can be seen are beacon lights and stars shining in the moonlit sky. Hannah rests her chin on her hands, gazing up at the illuminated night sky. She softly whispers, "A little guidance from the starry night, please," and with that, the taxi pulls onto the gravel drive, with the porch light guiding them home. Hannah notices the CCTV light is off. *Strange.* She's sure she rebooted it when she changed the code so Dylan couldn't watch. But it's too late for that. She figured she'd do it in the morning. She gently nudges Ruth. "Wakey, wakey, time to get to bed," but she protests like a child.

Chapter Twelve

YELLOW ROSES

The following day, Hannah felt like she had been hit by Cupid's naughty arrow. Why does she suddenly feel so besotted by this man? He's flashy and cheeky and not her type at all. *He looks like a movie star* - she keeps telling herself. It could be the smart red jacket, like a 30s smoking jacket, the handsome movie hunk from a time gone by. *Gosh Hannah,* she thought, this daydreaming needs to stop.

Sitting at the breakfast bar, she sips her coffee and looks out the window as she goes through everything in her mind again. Only this time she's not belittling herself, but telling herself off for fancying another bloke so quickly. The aroma of her yellow, fluffy jumper filled with lavender added to her contentment. A small smile crept onto her face as she thought to herself that the future was not so bad after all. There could be life after Dylan.

Suddenly, a loud thud echoes through the hallway as the post lands on the tiled floor, jolting Hannah out of her dream and back to reality. She quickly puts her coffee down and walks towards the front door, wishing she had the confidence to have given Harsmit her number instead of turning into a blabbering idiot. As she passes the guest room, the door was slightly ajar, so she peers inside and sees Ruth still sound asleep, sprawled out in the middle of the bed, fully dressed in a star shape. She hadn't moved an inch all night, it seems, and she closes the door quietly leaving her to sleep.

Hannah worries about Ruth's mental health. She seems all over the place at the moment and her state of mind is not as sharp as usual. Ruth was usually so strong and in control, but now she had fallen in love, something unexpected for her, and seems a mess without Zofia about. All Hannah wanted was for Ruth to be happy and in love. Zofia seemed to be the only girl she had ever seen Ruth look at twice since she has known her. However, speaking to Techy Ted would not be easy. Hannah remembers how she had come onto him in a drunken moment, but managed to stop before it went too far. But now, he was head over heels for her.

Bending down to pick up the post, Hannah notices a collection card. Someone had neglected to pay for postage, she thought to herself, but why would someone do that? She doesn't want the hassle of going to the busy collection office. It's always packed and only open at certain times. She put the card on the table by the door and thought of Dylan's warning about leaving her bag at the door in case someone broke in. She was about to take it upstairs but decides to put it back on the table. She felt like a rebel, defying him in some way. A satisfied look crosses her face as she mutters, "None of your business anymore."

An unexpected bang shook the front door. Peering through the glass, Hannah saw Martha, dressed in her usual wax coat and wellington boots and unkempt bush of hair. Martha has the traditional 'I'm wealthy but I don't care' look down to a T. Hannah wishes she would at least use a comb or put some straighteners on it. It looks like it has a life of its own at times. Taken aback that Martha has unexpectedly shown up at her door, it was clear that something was going on or someone was up to something. Martha wasn't the type to drop by for a cup of tea and a chat.

Hannah pulls open the heavy oak door and Martha just walks past her, as if the place belongs to her. "It took you long enough to answer. Do you usually just stand in the hallway staring into space?" Martha asks, taking off her boots and looking around the open plan room. "What I do in my own home is my business," Hannah replies, crossing her arms in defiance. "As far as I'm aware, this -," Martha gestures around the room, "-is still a company asset, but that doesn't matter right now. I just wanted to have a quick word; we haven't spoken in a while." The last thing Hannah wanted was for Martha to tell her how things should be. She just hoped Ruth wouldn't wake up as she might punch her lights out, so she needed to get Martha out of there as soon as possible.

"I wanted to apologise for what I said at the funeral," declares Martha. *Fuckin knock me down,* Hannah thinks. *Martha Burnside is apologising; I wish I had this on camera.* Intrigued, Hannah settles herself down on the sofa, Martha sits across on the high-back chair as the sofa is too low for her bad knee. "It was not my place to say and although things have ended, I have always seen you as a daughter. You see, I want the best for both of you and I just thought a clean break was the answer." Hannah's still in shock over the apology. "Well say something. Can you forgive an old woman?" Martha has a pleading look to her, but the devil comes in all shapes and sizes.

"To be honest, Martha." Hannah scratches her chin, trying to think of a response. "Maybe you were right. The wrong time to say it, but perhaps, but you were right. We should file the papers and start afresh." The words are flowing out of her mouth, but Hannah can't quite believe she's the one saying them. Who is this woman speaking and agreeing with Martha? "Excellent." Martha stands up to leave. "I will speak to the lawyers and make arrangements."

"Gran, didn't expect you to be here." Eva strides in with a huge bouquet of yellow roses, Hannah's favourite flowers.

"Have you been buying yourself roses again?" Eva asks her Mum. The card states 'Halifax Hannah, keep smiling and be happy. Love H'. Hannah squirms as Martha and Eva gaze at her for an answer. "Indeed, a lady should have the option to treat herself now and again," Hannah answers, getting the flowers from Eva and trying to hide her smile. Harsmit likes her. Oh, she is being so childish.

"Well said," Martha concurs. Hannah wished the ground would swallow her up. In any case, she quickly stops and turns to Eva. "What are you doing here? Why aren't you at Uni?" She senses something isn't right with Eva. Eva lowers her head attempting to muster up some courage. "I quit!" She states fearlessly. Eva looks over to Martha, who is shaking her head and back to her Mum.

"Oh no, you haven't given up, you're just taking a break." Hannah is trying to contain her annoyance but seeing Martha's 'I told you so' expression is making her more annoyed. "It's my life, it's not for you or Dad to decide. It's not for me and I won't go back and listen to all the nonsense they teach there." Eva is now frantic.

"I won't stand for it, Eva. you're intelligent and have so much potential. You have been talking about this course since you were in primary school." Hannah wasn't expecting this. Eva always seems so sure of her direction in life. "A person can be wrong, but you're too busy dealing with your own issues to see what I need," Eva shouts.

Hannah feels like she just got hit in the face with a brick. Eva grabs her walking boots and hurries out the door. Hannah attempts to follow her, but Martha blocks her. "Let her cool off, she's young and hot-headed, just like her Dad," says Martha. "She'll come to her senses and be back before you know it." Martha puts on her wellies and walks out to her Range Rover. What kind of day is this where Martha seems to be full of good advice?

Hannah looks back at the flowers on the table. Eva is right - too many bad decisions have been made lately. Maybe it's time to assess her decisions and take things slowly and consider Eva's feelings. It must be hard for her to see her parents fighting. She may be a young, determined woman with her own hopes and dreams, but Eva will always be Hannah's baby girl.

Chapter Thirteen

SHEEP SHIT SHOES

The energy in the house feels weird. Martha and Eva are gone. Having stared at the beautiful yellow roses for ten minutes, Hannah second guesses them like they are standing trial. She pulls at her chest and breathes hard and deep, a moment of bliss and now these golden buds look weathered to her. She's a bad person, an awful Mum. How could she do this? To want for herself and neglect others. The flowers are taunting her now, looking so perfect, but all the time remaining false. An illusion of happiness.

Hannah suddenly lunges towards them and starts bashing them on the counter. The petals flying everywhere as she takes out her anger on the unsuspecting bouquet. "I am an idiot," she shouts. "Easily bought with flowers." She drops to the ground with her head in her hands. Ruth, barley awake, comes running out of the room. She sees is Hannah on her knees on the kitchen floor and showers of yellow petals raining down around her. She towers over Hannah as she cowers on the floor. Ruth looks around to see if anyone else is in the house. "I feel like I may have missed something," she says with her hand on heart to steady her panic.

"Oh yes, you've missed something alright," Hannah replies, wiping snot from her nose. "From Dylan?" asks Ruth. Hannah lets out a small laugh. "Techy Ted, perhaps." Ruth doesn't have much to go on here.

Hannah closes her eyes and lets out another scream. "Okay, back out of the twilight zone," Ruth says, grabbing Hannah off the floor and shaking her. "What the fuck is going on, Han? I sleep in and you're killing harmless flowers." Hannah walks towards the cupboard and calmly grabs a brush and starts sweeping the petals up from the floor. "Martha has just been round," she says without looking up from the floor. "That's enough to push anyone over the edge." Ruth puts her hand over Hannah's hand and stops her moving the brush. Looking up at Ruth with tears in her eyes, she says, "I have single handily messed up Eva's life," and sobs a little more.

"Did Martha say that?" enquires Ruth.

"No, Eva has just been here, quitting Uni and it's my fault for being too wrapped up in my own problems." She throws the brush to the floor and Ruth grabs her and reassuringly rubs her arms.

"Now, let's get one thing straight. You're not a crap Mum. You are in fact the best, so let's go find Eva and sort this out. At her age, we all think we're invincible, but we still need our Mums. I know you didn't have that, but you wanted it didn't you?" Hannah nods in agreement drying her tears. "Okay, to the 'Hannah-Mobile'," orders Ruth.

H annah tries to call, text and leave voice mails on Eva's phone, but she's not answering. The only thing she can think of is to call Dylan and see if he's spoken to her. "What about that Ed bloke?" Suggested Ruth. "She's very friendly with him of late. He'll know exactly where she is. I bet he does."

"I don't have his number, or I would," replies Hannah.

"No need," Ruth winks at her. "He's there on that tractor." Ruth points to the green tractor turning over soil in the bottom fields. Hannah climbs the dry-stone wall and starts waving her hands as she walks towards Ed. From a distance it looks like Eva, so Ed jumps out and lights up a cig and swaggers towards her. After two puffs he realises it's not Eva. "Mrs B I thought yah was Eva, pretty strange considering I just dropped her off at the train station ten minutes ago," he says, taking another puff. "Halifax?" Hannah says really fast. He nods. That was much easier than Hannah thought it was going to be. Suppose Ed doesn't really know what's just happened. She thanks him and climbs back up the muddy bank.

They race though the lunchtime traffic, but it's like every red light was meant for them and the car also starts to smell of shit.

"Bloody hell." Ruth makes a choking noise and gags.

"I didn't have time to take me boots off," Hannah says, not taking her eyes off the road, thinking she must have stepped in some in the field. Ruth is checking train times on her phone. "Nothing to Kings Cross for another 10 mins so we should make it. She looks out for speed cameras and Hannah isn't slowing down.

"What the fuck does she think Dylan can do that I can't?" asks Hannah.

"It's probably not like that, she's just a runner like her father," sniggers Ruth. Hannah isn't amused by Ruth's comments.

The car bounces over the cobbles at the station, and Hannah stops the car and abandons it near the bike park. They look for the platform and run down the steps, hoping the train isn't early. "Eva, Eva," Hannah shouts, panicking she's missed her. "Show yer self, yah wee twat." Ruth spins around, shouting. People are looking at them and whispering to each other. They must look like two crazy ladies.

Eva appears from the coffee stand with her backpack and stares at them both, embarrassed. "I'm going to London, like it or not," she says, sipping her coffee smugly, sure of her decision. Hannah calms herself and gives Eva a big hug, nearly knocking the coffee all over her chest. "I am so sorry, my sweet girl," Hannah kisses her forehead. "You just caught me off guard and you're right, I wasn't seeing the signs that you had become unhappy." Eva pushes her away slightly and looks down at her zip top to make sure nothing has spilt. "Mum, I hate it, and nobody asks me what I really wanted. They all presume I will get over hating it. I don't want to be a solicitor like Dad. You all just presumed and packed me off to Uni." Eva's face looks lost, like a little five-year-old looking for answers. Hannah doesn't know the answer, she just doesn't want her baby to feel like this.

"London will not give you answers. Stay here with me. You could bring Ed round for dinner one night," Hannah says. "You said it was lambing season soon and sounded excited to get your hands dirty." She looks at Eva longingly. Eva puts her coffee on the top of the bin and puts her backpack back on. "No, I don't expect answers, I just want to be away for a bit, and let's face it Dad's not going to be around," she shrugs her shoulders, kisses her Mum on the cheek, picks up her coffee and boards the train. "Call me anytime," Hannah shouts at the train window. Eva pops her headphones in and gives a small wave. Hannah watches her thinking her little girl is all grown up.

Ruth's standing at the car as Hannah walks back and points at the windscreen. "You got a ticket."

"No shit, Sherlock," barks Hannah as she rips the yellow sticker off the window and throws it onto the cobbles. They get in the car and drive in silence for a few minutes, then Ruth starts messing with the radio channels. "Leave it alone," she says through gritted teeth. "Chill, Han," Ruth slaps her on the hand as they both fight for the radio channel. They burst out laughing. "One thing after another," sighs Hannah. "Bet it was that prick Councillor Jeremy with the ticket. Probably stalking you about Halifax," Ruth implies.

"Am I a bad Mum?" Hannah asks Ruth.

"No, you are just a Mum and sometime Mums have to shovel shit, but you do it and get on," Ruth twitches her nose. "Speaking of shit, I think we best stop at the car wash and bin those bloody boots," she points to Hannah's feet.

"I need a drink," Hannah says, defeated.

"Not me," Ruth declines.

"You're still queasy?" asks Hannah suspiciously.

Ruth rolls down the window and inhales the fresh, moist air. "Yes, and your shitty shoes are not helping, so let's get that sorted first, then you can drown your sorrows." She tries to deflect but can see Hannah is hurt by her comments. "If you're good, I will make you one of my Irn Bru slushies laced with vodka." She rolls her eyes at Hannah. Ruth knows that Hannah can't say no to a vodka slushy from the old days. Hannah beams and is suddenly very cheery about the slushy offer.

Chapter Fourteen

SAVING YOUR OWN SKIN

Eva stands in the middle of her Dad's London flat, finding it hard not to be disappointed. "Dad, you live in a box." She does a 360-degree turn. "Everything is at touching distance, it's bizarre." She feels out with both hands wiggling her fingers. Eva then thrusts her hips toward the toilet. "I could literally pee from the lounge seat, and it would hit the toilet pan." She can't stop laughing. All this time she thought he was living a high-end London life and instead he's staying in a shoebox.

Dylan, on the other hand, is looking a little uneasy. He wasn't expecting a visit. "It's just me, so not much room in my man pad." He stands up from the brown leather armchair. "Don't worry, I'm not planning on staying permanently!" Eva says in a huffy voice as she can't believe he said the words 'man pad'. "Oh, I didn't mean it like that love." Dylan had put his foot in it. He pops the kettle on, and Eva starts messing with the television channels, looking for music.

He hands her the brew. "I had plans for the day, but I'm sure I can rearrange, but I do need to pop the office for a bit, too." His meeting with Claire is today and he wants Eva nowhere near it. If she or Hannah found out, they would not understand his reasons for going. "I don't mind coming to the office, I'll get to see the busy city life of yours," she says sarcastically. Dylan can't resist asking about Hannah. "How's

Mum?" he asks nervously after Eva has taken a few sips of her tea. She looks up at him. "Do you really want to know the answer to that?" She's surprised by his question but too busy pulling faces at her brew which doesn't taste right.

"Just checking in. Has she been feeling well?" If Eva says she's been sick recently, that confirms pregnancy as Hannah couldn't hold a thing down with Eva during the first trimester. Not wanting her Dad to know about the fight she just had with her Mum, she says, "No she's good, even sending herself flowers." She shook her head at the tea. "This is like pish water! Tastes awful." With that, she heads to the sink and pours it away. "You sound like Ruth 'pish water.'" He mocks in a Scottish accent. "She does rub off on you," Eva laughs.

"The water down south isn't the same, but you get used to it." He goes to grab his phone from the side table. "Let's head to the office and I will show you where the magic happens," Dylan says and opens the door. "Please don't say that ever again, Dad," Eva pleads with him. Dylan looks embarrassed but just laughs at her.

The Brixton-based office is near to the flat. It's above a charity shop and split over two floors, with around ten staff members working in this branch of the Burnside Holdings London site. They have three branches in total, of which two are in England, and one in Paisley outside Glasgow in Scotland. Evidently, that is how Dylan met Ruth. He was at Glasgow Uni while Ruth and he both worked part time at the Paisley branch. They dated until they both met Hannah at a rave. It was the full-on 90s rave scene at the Tunnel in Glasgow. Dylan knew in that moment that Hannah was who he wanted. He had never been so mesmerised by one person. The way she danced with the strobe lights extenuating her blonde hair and white mesh top. She looked like a goddess to him then and even now.

He suspected Ruth was gay, but it wasn't until her friendship blossomed with Hannah that Ruth felt comfortable being herself. Dylan suspected Ruth had feelings for Hannah as she always wanted to spend time with her. However, he came to realise in time they both had developed a solid friendship, with one always needing the other. Yes, it's love at its strongest, a true friendship based on trust and honesty. They both see each other's strengths and weaknesses and celebrate both. A bond Dylan was always jealous of but could never compete with.

E va goes straight to the coffee machine in the staff area. She is desperate for a decent latte, but not convinced after this morning's brew of pish. Meanwhile, Dylan is frantically walking back and forth about in his office. He needs to message Claire, but what if she threatens to turn up if he doesn't see her. He starts to type but Eva comes in the door. "Look at you and your swanky London office space! Not quite the dingy digs in Halifax," she says, looking at the high loft ceilings. "Halifax has history." Dylan pops his phone back into his pocket. "Is that brew to madam's taste?" He points to the large mug Eva is sipping from. She sits on the egg-shaped chair in the corner.

"Aye, it will do."

A male voice can be heard from the hallway. "Didn't know you were coming in, Mr Burnside?". Sam, the office apprentice, appears in the doorway. He leans against it and looks Eva up from head to toe. She smirks back and continues to sip her coffee. "Sam, this is my daughter, Eva." Dylan introduces them. Excellent, he thinks to himself, Sam can distract Eva. "Can you give Eva a tour of the building while I make a few calls?" Sam stands up straight and eagerly waves Eva over.

"Would be my pleasure," he turns to Dylan, full of smiles. Eva doesn't mind, he's easy on the eye and she's bored.

Once the office is clear, Dylan closes the door. He calls Claire instead, as he's not sure of her reaction on text. It's her voice mail. "Hi

Claire, something has come up and I need to rearrange. Text you later." He hangs up and catches his breath, feeling panicked. But his phone beeps with a message straight away. It says 'We meet, or I come to London today. I need to talk and refuse to wait any longer. Claire.' He taps the phone on his forehead several times swearing to himself. No way can he allow Eva and Claire to see each other. He must think of a plan to stop Claire from making her way to London.

He begins typing. 'Claire, I will meet you as planned at 5pm in Kent, please forward me the address. Do not come to London. I will come to you as promised. Dylan.' He closes his eyes and hopes that does the trick and presses send. Full of fear, he stares for a reply and can see she is typing. The message comes through. '5pm Café Royal. Please be there. Claire.' Sweat forms on the back of his neck. So much guilt is rushing through his entire body, and he shakes. Reaching for his office fridge, he takes out a can of energy drink and nearly drinks it in one go.

"That stuff is pretty bad for you, Dad." Eva stood at the office door is shaking her head at him like she's the parent. "Will do my best to cut back, Mum," he answers in a baby voice.

"Sam's proper fit! In a 'Made In Chelsea' kinda way." Eva is eyeing him up as Sam is sitting at his desk pretending not to look at her.

"Hmm." Dylan doesn't want to encourage Eva but admits this could be the diversion he needs in order to get that train to Kent without arousing suspicion.

"Well, if he's that fit, let's see what the lad is up to tonight then," he declares and walks towards Sam, who's looking nervous as Dylan approaches him with a determined look. "Sam, Eva's not really seen the sights of London, and she doesn't want her old man dragging her around. I am sure you know all the hidden spots this city has to offer," he leans over the desk, as he's not really asking more telling.

"Yes, sir, I do but..." Sam is unsure how to answer.

"So how about you take my girl around for the rest of the day on me?" Dylan then produces the company credit card and slides it across the table. Sam's eyes light up likes its Christmas Day. "I would be honoured to." Sam then turns to Eva. "That's if it's okay with you? I do know all the hidden music and book shops we could look at and then grab some roof top drinks." Eva is a little taken aback, normally Dad doesn't seem so keen on blokes taking her out and now he seems to be paying someone to do so. She becomes suspicious but can't be arsed with her parents at the moment, so replies. "Well, if Daddy wants to pay, I would be delighted to."

"Settled then." Dylan slaps his hand on the table and walks towards his office. "I will head off now and leave you young ones to it. Becoming a boring old man these days and going to catch up on today's footie." He attempts to laugh at himself but can tell Eva is not convinced. She walks over to Sam, who is still sitting at his desk with the credit card in his hands, staring at it like it's the golden ticket. She sits on the desk and suggestively slides her hand down Sam's back while looking up at her Dad to gauge his reaction. "Yes, Sammy, let's go and spend Daddy's money," she says sarcastically. Sam is oblivious as he can't take his eyes off the card in his hands. Dylan's not even looking at them, he seems more preoccupied with leaving.

Dylan puts on his jacket and then checks his phone for any messages from Claire. He looks up at Eva and Sam. "Enjoy guys," he attempts to be cheery. Walking down the stairs, he looks back at his daughter. He knows what he has just done is wrong and starts to judge himself harshly. Well, what a guy you are, Dylan Burnside, selling out your own flesh and blood to save your skin.

Chapter Fifteen

TECHY TERRITORY

The parking in Halifax town centre is unbearable. They closed the best car parks to build flats and provided no extra parking. Hannah drives around looking for a safe place to park, but it's always the same on a weekday. It's like everyone is out and about today and all she needs to do is pick up the stupid parcel that needs paying for. If she finds the person who sent it, she could hit them with it right now.

Giving up on trying to park as close as possible to the sorting office, she then makes her way down to the train station car park, as there's always a space there. She can just walk up and have a little browse through the Piece Hall on her way back. A bonus to the day, plus she can leave her window slightly open down there. Her car might have been cleaned, but it still smells of shit.

However, this means walking past Techy Ted's shop, and as much as she promised Ruth to speak to him about finding Zofia, she can't quite bring herself to walk in there, a little ashamed of her actions. Luckily, the shop is in darkness as she approaches, and a sign on the door says it's closed for lunch. Hannah writes him a note and puts Ruth's details on it, and this way, hopefully, he will help her out instead of dismissing Hannah for going a little weird on him. But come on, she thinks, she has been going through a rough time.

The sorting office doesn't seem to have a large queue and luckily, she has made it on time before it closes. The lady at the counter makes no eye contact and instead is sitting whilst on her phone. Hannah hands over the collection note, her ID, and her bank card. The lady behind the counter searches for a few moments and the produces a small jiffy back. Hannah has a little flashback. She hates the vanilla bags. Reminds her of the day she opened those horrible photos of Claire and Dylan. A sight she shall never forget. She takes it and walks to the exit.

Turning it over, she sees the postage address is Halifax. Very strange. Who would just post something from the same town. Bizarre she thinks to herself. As she leaves, she walks straight into Techy Ted. "Are you following me?" Ted runs his hand nervously through his quaffed hair. Hannah pops the envelope in her bag. Oh, God, what does she say. This is so awkward. "Techy, I mean Ted, nice to see you." That's all she can muster up. "I was doing Pilates in the park on my lunch break, just stretching the pelvis out." He flexes his groin out, talking very fast and appears to be nervous.

"Okay." That's not weird much. "I've left you a note at the shop." Hannah is so uncomfortable as he is still flexing his groin.

"A note? Are we Romeo and Juliet Now?" He runs his hand through his hair again and nervously laughs out loud. "No, not like that, it's from Ruth." Hannah tried to make this less awkward than it already is. She needs to get out of here. "I need to shoot, so will talk later." She touches his shoulder and can see him blush with excitement. She rushes off towards the Piece Hall leaving Techy Ted chatting to himself in the window. It's ridiculous. How is she going to let him down gently? She shall set Ruth on him, that will terrify him.

Hannah walks through the entrance to the Piece Hall, looking round to make sure Ted hasn't followed her and heads straight to the bookshop. It's a safe place for her. Techy Ted prefers his computers. Nothing better than finding new books, interesting reads that can transport you to another world. Browsing for a while as there's so much choice, she sets her heart on a little short story based on a local woman who worked at the chocolate factory and ignores the self-help section as she has had her fill of them.

Book purchased, and placed in a little brown eco-friendly bag, she walks out the shop when her phone rings. It's Eva. "Mum, I'm on my way back. I know I only just got here. But the Big Smoke is not for me." She doesn't want to tell her Mum about being fobbed off to Sam who was only too happy to take Dylan's card and dump her. "And Ed says the lambs are due and I want to be there to help out, so you'll probably see me till tomorrow. I get into Halifax later on." The phone is breaking up as she's on the train. "Okay, baby, I missed you and hope at least had a good time with your Dad." Hannah is all smiles again knowing her baby is back and the fact that it was short meant that she didn't want to stay. "Mum, I will see you..." And with that, the phone cuts off.

Hannah sits down on a bench in the open courtyard and sends Eva a quick text just to make sure she's okay. She looks around at the stunning venue she's sitting in. It could be mistaken for an Italian square as the sun lights up the building. The Hall is very rustic and well looked after. One of the most well-preserved buildings in Halifax and a draw for visitors all over the world.

A new bar has opened, offering wine and tapas. She grabs a table in the sun and puts her sunglasses on, absorbing its rays. Ordering a dry white wine, olives and a cheese board, Hannah takes out the strange jiffy and opens it for a look. Her phone rings again and, presuming it is Eva, she answers quickly, using her posh telephone voice.

"Hello darling, have you got better service now?" The voice she hears back is male. "Well, darling this is very formal."

Oh no! She holds her hand over her mouth. It's Harsmit. What does she say? "I am so sorry, I thought it was my daughter Eva." Why do these things happen to her? It goes quiet for a second. "Hello," she says again. "I just wanted to hear that posh voice again, Halifax Hannah." Harsmit is laughing. "Did you receive my flowers?" Shit! The flowers that she battered all over the kitchen in a mega meltdown. "Yes, very lovely, and thank you. Sorry I didn't message you and thank you, I didn't have your number," she says, hoping he never finds out about the massacre that happened with those poor petals.

"Would it be okay if I invited you for dinner in Leeds? I would like to see you again if it's something you would like?" His tone is no longer jokey but soft and wanting. What's a girl to do. She promised herself to have more control and not go in headfirst when she hears a male heartbeat. "Harsmit, firstly, I am flattered, and I do want to meet. In fact, I would very much like to. But I promised myself to be more careful with whom I see from now on. I am prone to going in headfirst..." He interrupts her.

"Hannah, it really is just dinner, nothing more." She hears him sigh slightly. "I understand, but I promise it's just two grownups having a chat." He used the word grownups so how could she resist. He didn't need to twist her arm. "Okay, two grownups will meet in Leeds and have a chat," she says firmly.

"That's an official dinner and a chat then," laughs Harsmit. "Tomorrow night, say about 6pm and I will meet you at the station." He's being very precise. "Tomorrow it is then." She picks up the glass of wine and puts her phone in her jacket pocket. The sun warms her face again, and she decides to create a checklist for herself to keep her on some kind of track. One to which she must always adhere.

Hannah's good behaviour list created for good emotional wellbeing:
1 Do not drink on too many weekdays.
2 Stop eating takeaways.
3 Avoid negativity. (Stay away from Martha)
4 Don't have sex on the first date.
5 Don't crave love from unhealthy sources.
6 Most importantly - take things slowly.

Perhaps if she follows a few simple rules, everyone wins. Then again, who is she kidding? She has been let down by everything she has held dear these last eight months so they can all go fuck themselves, she thinks and downs the last drop of her wine.

"Excuse me," she shouts to the woman taking orders. "Can I please see your wine menu and dessert one too?" She stares at the wine glass and back out at all the people scurrying about the place enjoying a little bit of sun. She sees everyone getting on with life and thinks that's what she'll do. I'm no different to anyone else, it's all about moving forward, she thinks. However, she spots Techy Ted wandering across the middle of the court. He doesn't seem to notice her. So, with that, she grabs her wine and heads inside to look for a table and hides in case he comes back. She wasn't proud of it, and she supposed the self-help books did nothing for her. Oh, but wait, 'live to fight another day'. Maybe she learned something after all.

Chapter Sixteen

SPILT TEA

For once, the London trains are on time despite getting to the station early just in case. Having caught the 3.30pm to Kent, Dylan is hoping there'll be no delays and he'll make good time so he can get back to Eva, as he's now consumed with guilt for leaving her with Sam. The conductor is making a few announcements, but everything is on time. He sits back and catches his breath. A small child is staring at him and making him think back to little baby Eva, so tiny and helpless and how he's just left her.

He holds his head in his hands hoping for some kind of divine intervention to guide him, but as usual, nothing has been on his side so far this year. "We are now stopping at 'Strood,'" the voice calls from the Tanoy. He makes sure he has his phone and jacket and heads off the train quickly. It's a small station, and he gets out his phone for directions to the café Claire has confirmed as the meeting point. It says a five-minute walk away and so his timing is good as he'd like to get there before Claire to feel more at ease.

The weather is still slightly warm and he takes his jacket off. He follows the voice directions on his phone and tries to clear his head before the confrontation. He looks up and down the street and can see the small café on the right-hand side, it has blurred windows and lots of purple flowers surrounding the door entrance. Dylan goes to walk in, but notices Claire is already sitting there looking for him while nervously playing with a mug. She hasn't seen him yet, and he steps back from the door and moves out of view. He can feel his heart racing, even looking at her, knowing he can't believe he went there.

He needs to calm himself down and not let her see his emotions. He still has no recollection of them being together and thinks she wants some kind of payoff. He can only image that Martha originally paid her to leave the valley soon after the pictures were discovered. He presumed she had perhaps gone with Richard, but he is yet to answer Dylan's millions of calls and messages.

Claire looks up from her drink and can see Dylan hovering and does a gentle wave to encourage him in. Dylan can't go back now, so he pushes through the door and sits across from her with his hands clasped on the table. "Would you like a drink or maybe a glass of water?" she looks towards the counter smiling briefly, but full of nerves, "No, do you need another one?" he asks clearing his throat and trying not to look her in the eye. They both sit in silence for a few seconds. Each wondering how the other is going to react and who is going to speak first.

But Dylan can't take it anymore and breaks the ice first. Her silence is killing him. "What do you want Claire, more money? Hannah knows so you can say all you want to her." He throws his hands down at his sides in defeat. She looks across at him and Dylan is surprised to see a look of sorrow on her face as her eyes begin to tear up. She looks completely lost. For a moment he feels sorry for her and looks down at her arms as she pulls her sleeves down. "I am sorry for all I have put you and Hannah through," she sniffs and wipes a tear from her cheeks. "I truly am, and I do not want any money from you. I especially want nothing to do with your family, particularly that idiot Richard."

"Wait," says Dylan who's now unsure of what is happening here. "You left with Richard. He cleaned some of our accounts out and hasn't been seen since." Claire slams her hand down hard on the table and it shakes, sending some of her tea onto it. "He is a liar and bully and I hope he rots in hell. All of this- everything -is his fault," she sobs. People start looking at the table. Dylan hands her a napkin and leans over and tries to comfort her. He doesn't want people to think there's a problem. She blows her nose hard into the napkin.

Poking her finger into the spilt tea on the table, Claire continues, "You see, I am a bad person or, so I was before. I need to clear my sins from my head and it's part of my recovery programme to face my fears." Guilt is all Dylan now feels. What has he done to this girl?

"And I am one of your fears?" Dylan is now really confused.

"What I did to you and how low I stooped for some cash or what I thought was some kind of love is my fear. I must face what I have done." Claire is trying to control her crying. "We had sex, Claire, and that's that," declares Dylan. Suddenly she seems to get a little more control of herself. She looks somewhat apologetic. "You see, that's the thing," Claire closes her eyes. "We didn't have sex, Dylan!" She blurts out.

He stares at her whilst tapping his finger on the table. What did she just say? Is this a game? Is she lying or recording something?

"Say something Dylan," begs Claire.

"What do you mean we didn't have sex? There were pictures." A lump of sick jumps into his throat and there's sweat on his neck again. "You had been drinking and Richard found you out cold on the office floor. He called me to come help as we were going to go for a curry, said we could drop you off at yours on the way." She stops and can no longer look at Dylan. "And what?" Dylan is impatient now; anger burns inside him. "He suggested I take my clothes off and take some pics with you. He said it would be easy money and that he was only sending them to Martha's phone. He said she would pay good money to get them deleted." Biting her nails and sliding down her chair, Claire explains, "I was at a very low point. I thought he liked me, and I could pay off some bills with the money, so I did it." More tears flow down her face, but Dylan doesn't feel sorrow for her anymore.

"So, you and Richard set me up and sent them to Hannah instead?" She looks surprised at that accusation. "No, as far as I am aware he sent them to Martha. He appeared a couple of days later with a load of cash, more than I could count, and said it was best to leave and he would come to Kent and meet me, but he never did." She then stands up and takes her bag. "You see, he was obsessed with Martha and hated you for some reason." Claire can barely speak. "That's all I had to and wanted to say, I am not looking for you to forgive me because as yet I can't forgive myself. I promise this is the last time you will hear from me." Walking towards Dylan, who's trying to absorb all this information, she puts her hand on his shoulder and says, "I am truly sorry." He shrugs his shoulder away from her hand and she slowly walks out the door, looking back at him full of shame.

The waitress approaches the table, but Dylan takes no notice as he's still not sure what has just happened and why it happened. "Sir, sir," the waitress leans in front of his face. "The lady has left without paying for her tea. It's £3.75, please, if you don't mind paying considering the drama that been happening at this table." She puts out her hand demanding payment. Dylan throws a £20 on the table, stands up and says nothing.

He makes his way back to the station, pushing through people and taking no notice of what's in front of him. Every part of his body is swollen with rage, his life with Hannah has been blown apart for nothing because of some bloke's sad obsession with his mother. Everything always boils down to Martha. He's even sure his father began to hate her in old age. His phone beeps and it's a message from Eva. It reads: 'Where are you, Dad? Cos I am going back home.'

Chapter Seventeen

GINGER LIPS

Hannah is all about her accountant duties today, since Ruth has ordered far too much stock. She needs to put the 'Sale of the Century' together on the website to try to make some money back. This is her primary source of income now, and she can no longer rely on the Burnside funds to help her out. She knows that Dylan won't be too gentle in the divorce if Martha has her way. Glancing at her phone, she notices ten missed calls from Dylan, but no messages. She assumes it's because of Eva coming home early, and as far as she's concerned, it's his problem. Daddy cannot buy her love anymore. This makes her incredibly happy.

It looks like Eva is now starting to feel good about herself, and that makes Hannah very proud. Unfortunately, the business bank account is not in the best shape due to the ever-increasing costs of Council Tax, rent, gas and electricity, not to mention online subscriptions and advertising. Hannah looks towards the toilet. Ruth has been in the bathroom for most of the morning. Her outlandish spending has not helped with the increasing overhead costs. Hannah is fed up with insisting she go to the doctor for her stomach bug. Ruth finally comes out looking a bit better and grabs a pack of ginger biscuits, gobbling down as many as she can fit in her mouth.

Hannah can't stand the crunching noise. "Slow down, you'll bring them up in five mins if you're not careful." Ruth pulls a face and bites hard into her biscuit. "So, Little-Miss-Moody-Pants," she says, pulling another from the packet and sitting on a stool next to Hannah. "Big date tonight with Braders Boy?" she inspects her biscuit like it the finest thing she has ever seen. "It's not a date, it's a friendly chat." Hannah shrugs off Ruth's accusations and is very quick to make her aware of that. "You like him, you can't hide it from me, Han." She tickles her waist. "Look at you, like a little teenager checking your phone and smiling at it. You're in love," Ruth Laughs and nearly chokes on a biscuit.

Hannah admits to herself that she does really like Harsmit. Something about new beginnings is so satisfying to her. It's the middle and the end that's genuinely the problem for her. Ruth starts tapping repeatedly on Hannah's arm in a panic. "Shit! Little Romeo is here," she whispers. "Harsmit is here?" Hannah looks up all cheery, but her face soon drops. Techy Ted stands in front of them at the shop counter. He seems to have been standing there for a few good minutes, silently watching and listening. "Hi, Techy," Ruth says, licking her biscuit. Techy Ted nods at Hannah and then turns his attention to Ruth. "Ruth, I have done some much needed digging, and located some of Zofia's family on social media in Poland. They live in a place called Jastrzebie-zdroj," he says politely while trying not to look at Hannah.

Ruth chucks the biscuits down and grabs the bit of paper Ted is holding. They have a little struggle back and forth and he then grudgingly let's go. She kisses him smack on the lips. He wipes the biscuit from his lips. "Mm ginger, not one of my favourites," he says while getting sanitiser out to clean his hands. Ruth skims over the paper and cannot contain her joy. She runs upstairs with the paper like a woman possessed to access the upstairs computer away from prying eyes, leaving Hannah alone with Techy Ted in the shop.

"I want to say something," Hannah says, breaking the silence, but he goes up to her and puts his finger on her mouth and shushes her. "Hannah, I have come to believe that you may have used me in an attempt to make yourself feel happy at a low moment in your midlife crisis." He looks at her for confirmation and also as if he is in some way telling her off. Hannah nods as no words enter her head to reply to poor Techy Ted. "This was unkind, and I may have got a little carried away dreaming of us running a little S & M shop in Lanzarote. Sunny all year round," he puts his thumbs up and then looks at the floor and mutters, "well I may have told a few people that on the internet anyway." Hannah is puzzled and weirded out by it all.

"Look, you are right, and I did use you. For that I am sorry as you seem like a nice guy." Even though after that confession she's not sure of that. "Oh no Hannah, don't apologise. No need, I am happy to be of use to you. Since I posted my story online, I've been contacted by loads of unhappy ladies and some men wanting a little 'Ted Time'," he grins like he has won the lottery.

"'Ted Time', I see." Hannah thinks she's created a monster and smiles at him, hoping he'll soon leave. "Well, I wish you all the best with your internet dating, Ted." Hannah doesn't know how to react to this information or whether she wants to laugh or cry. "I wonder, to remember our last moment between us, can I take a little something from the shop? As a memory?" He eyes up the merchandise and walks over to a gimp suit in 'The Last Chance To Buy' section. "Been after one of these bad boys for a while," he winks at Hannah, and with his suit under his arm, whistles as he leaves the shop and happily strolls down the street.

Hannah stands behind the counter completely gobsmacked and to think he seemed like a shy lad. What the hell has she done to him? He didn't even ask for a bag to put the suit in. Ruth comes flying down the stairs, waving the bit of paper in front of Hannah's face. "Is Romeo gone?". She looks about for Ted.

"Oh, he's well gone!" Hannah replies, still in shock.

"So, I have messaged a few people who might know where she's gone, but it's in Polish, and I need your help with Google Translate." Ruth's eyes are like big chocolate buttons begging for help.

"Okay, but anyone can use that now, but quickly, then I need to get home and get ready for my big chat date." Hannah's not looking at what she's been writing with and puts the vag pen in her mouth.

"You just like a vag, don't you really" Ruth teases

"Shut up, do you want my help or not?

Ruth keeps teasing her, "Vag, oh vag. Han likes vag." Hannah hits her with her pen.

Ruth looks over at 'The Last Chance' section. "Did we sell that awful gimp suit today?" she looks surprised as it's been there for months.

"Don't even ask," Hannah says.

"But I promised it to Ella next door for one of her photo shoots." Ruth seems pretty miffed. She goes over and rummages in the basket. "Oh, thank you. People, we have winner," she says, holding it in the air and waving it. "I wouldn't exactly call it a winner, Ruth. More like another bad purchase." Hannah snaps at her. She really wishes Ruth would make some proper business decisions, instead of buying on a whim. "Now, now sarky pants. You just think of that nice date tonight and those brown puppy-dog eyes glistening over the candlelight, wanting nothing but a piece of Hannah's arse," she slaps the suit on the front desk and places it in a reusable gift bag. "Do not sell this! It's for Ella."

"Yes, ma'am," Hannah salutes her and turns off her laptop.

"So, what time's the train? I just need five mins for translation and then you can have a pre-date bath." Ruth bosses Hannah to the upstairs computer. She sets up Google Translate and shows Ruth how to work it, knowing Ruth can do it herself but is a little afraid of technology. "Don't spend too long chatting, just find out locations. You don't want her thinking you're stalking her and scare her off again." Hannah says this without thinking. Ruth doesn't get angry though and says, "That was low even for you, Han." Hannah sits next to her.

"I just seem to be saying sorry a lot recently, but I truly am. Do what you've got to do, and I will be right by your side," she punches Ruth's arm. "Well, not tonight, obviously."

Chapter Eighteen

CHAT DATE

Hannah looks up at the train times. The second train is now delayed from Halifax to Leeds. No issue with Manchester, so why is it always the Leeds side? This always happens when she decides to get a train. Hannah texts Harsmit to let him know she may be late and is now going to grab a taxi instead. Dashing out of the train station, she sees a taxi and grabs it before someone else does.

"Leeds Train Station, please and don't take the M62 or we'll be car-parked for hours," she explains. As the taxi pulls up to turn right at the lights, she sees Martha standing outside the Business Council office with Davis Jeremy. They're in deep conversation so Hannah whips out her phone and tries to take a few pictures as the taxi now turns left instead and speeds off.

Hannah doesn't trust either of them. She's sure they're conspiring against her, and from now on she's going to document everything and anything in the run up to filing for divorce, which either party has yet to do. Martha is always out to get what she wants, and Dylan always lets her. Eva's face appears on the phone, she looks so cute Hannah thinks to herself that she didn't come home last night. These lambs are only an excuse. She answers the FaceTime.

Eva is ecstatic and a little messy looking, not as cute as the phone picture. "Mum, I delivered my first lamb, look!" she turns the phone to a baby lamb freshly birthed and its mother cleaning it down. "Oh, so cute," squeaks Hannah. "But put your phone down a bit lower. I can see blood on those gloves, and did you wear a mask?" Eva isn't bothered.

"Mum, live in the moment. I've sent you a video of the birth." Hannah screws up her face. "Oh, how kind of you." She holds back the sick feeling in her throat, it's not what she wants to be looking at right now. "See yah tomorrow and I will show you everything," and Eva blows her a kiss. Hannah hasn't seen her this happy in ages; covered head to toe in shit and blood, beaming from ear to ear.

Eva has sent another video that comes up on Hannah's phone and all she can see is Eva sticking her hand up the sheep's bum. "No, not for me, not before my meal," she says out loud and turns the video message off. The driver looks at her in the mirror and quickly puts his eyes back on the road. The taxi pulls up outside a big hotel next to the station as it's easier for the driver to get in and out of Leeds this way. Hannah rings Harsmit to find out exactly where he's waiting but he doesn't answer.

As she turns around to look, she can see a man approach her, singing and with a yellow rose in his hand. Oh, please help me she thinks. Holding her hands over her mouth, trying not to laugh he puts his hand out for her to take it. Hannah does so and can't stop smiling. He pulls her close and they slowly dance in a circle in the middle of the street. People are watching and taking pictures, and she's embarrassed, but the attention is kind of nice. "Now is this the kind of public chat you had in mind?" he smiles at her. Hannah rests her forehead on his shoulder, laughing. "Come on, Halifax Hannah, let's get comfy and we can chat until the sun comes up," he breaks away from her and leads her through the small crowd that has gathered.

The night sky can be seen in full beauty from the glass dome roof in the rooftop restaurant. They are seated in a private dining area with views of the city skyline. "You like the stars?" Will, the restaurant owner, asked. He is a business acquaintance of Harsmit who has come to greet them. Hannah can't stop looking up. "Yes, the roof is wonderful, and the space is amazing. I might need to visit my physio tomorrow from looking up," she laughs at herself.

"I thought that if you agree, we could try the taster menu and the wine flight," Harsmit interrupts.

"Yes, then we both venture anew," Hannah puts the menu down. "You read my mind. Look at us, adults chatting and agreeing."

He bends forward with his hands clasp and nods to Will to take the menus away. "So, Hannah, tell me about yourself," he begins.

"No," she interrupts. "Let's not talk about the past, let's just drink our wine and discuss our menu, like we are great food lovers."

"So, you want to play 'let's pretend'?" he leans back, intrigued. She sighs a little. "I just don't want to go over old ground. I don't want to go headfirst into something. I just want to enjoy your company but at a steady pace," she blurts all that out in one breath.

"I couldn't agree more and to start we let the waiter choose our first pre-meal drinks." Harsmit picks up his glass of water, "To friendship, chatting and new adventures," he says. Hannah taps her glass against his, blissfully lost in his gaze.

Five courses are brought out during the evening meal, each one paired with wine. They both chat like old school friends throughout the meal and both clear each plate, eagerly awaiting the next to arrive, however by the end Hannah is flagging behind. The hazelnut chocolate macaroons in raspberry sauce with a sweet dessert wine have finished her off, and she asks to take the course of cinder toffee pie home with her. The restaurant wraps the desserts and place them on the table. "Thank you for making me laugh." Hannah touches his hand.

"Halifax Hannah, it has been an honour and a privilege to experience this vast meal," he taps on his belly, "and to spend time with you this evening." He then turns her hand over and slightly tickles the palm of her hand. "I only wish it were longer, but the wine is starting to affect me. I will just nip to the loo and then we can get the bill." With this, Hannah stands up, and a little wobbly, makes her way to the bathroom.

Pulling her 'hold-me-in pants' down, she lands with a bang on the toilet seat. "Aww," she lets out a sigh of relief and feels for toilet roll, but there is none. "Fuck," she screeches out loud. Hovering over the pan, she tries to shake herself off. She then opens the toilet door and leans forward to make sure nobody's there. She then walks with her pants at her ankles, trying not to drip while searching for toilet roll in the next cubicle. "Result!" She slides down the wall on to the toilet seat.

Washing her hands, she tries to adjust her eye make-up in the mirror and put on some fresh lippy. Coming out from the bathroom, Harsmit stands waiting with her coat.

"What about the bill?" she says with one arm in the coat as he holds it.

"What about your lipstick. Did you ask the hand dryer to put it on?" he wipes the red smeared lipstick from her chin.

"Oh," she says.

"Let's get to the car and I'll drop you off in my taxi," he says, escorting her to the lift.

Hannah must've fallen asleep as the next thing the car has pulled up outside her house. "I am sorry, I must have dosed off," she sits up in the seat. "You may have slobbered slightly on my shoulder," Harsmit wipes it and laughs. "Oh god, I am so sorry," Hannah says, embarrassed again. "Nothing to be sorry about. You just needed a nana nap after our mammoth feast." He adjusts her hair from her face.

"Tonight, has been very different for me. I haven't felt this comfortable on a chatting date before," he leans his head to one side. "In fact, neither of us looked at our phones once and that's also a first for me." He takes both of her hands and kisses them. "Goodnight and I hope we can do this again at some point soon?"

"We can do this for certain." And with that, Hannah leans in and kisses him on those honey lips.

Chapter Nineteen

LAMB LOVE

M rs Thornes had spent the best part of the early hours making breakfast and hands them out to the hungry workers. She knows the crew needs a bit of fuel after a long day and night on the farm. It's 5am and Eva is completely knackered but still in high spirits. She sits on a stack of pallets with the others surrounded by a mixture of water, blood, and straw. Never in her young life has she enjoyed a breakfast as much as this morning. Her choice is sausage teacake smothered in brown sauce with a large mug of milky coffee.

The sun is rising, and the valley is slowly waking up to a new day. The air is slightly chilled, and the rain washes away last night's hard, long labours. Out amongst the fields are a few new editions to the world and they are settling next to their mummies for some comfort as they adjust to their new lives. Walking out into the field with her bright red wellies and warming her hands on her mug of fresh coffee, Eva lets out a big sigh. Not of sadness, or sorrow but a deep sense of fulfilment. Eva Burnside had a helping hand in bringing spring to the Shibden Valley and not everyone gets to participate, so she feels and sees the joy in that.

Ed, who had finished cleaning the barn, comes from behind, puts his arms around Eva and grasps the coffee mug she is holding for warmth. She holds it up to his mouth, and he takes a sip. "Look at us starting a cosy little family together," he grins and kisses her on cold cheeks. They both look at the lambs in the field like proud parents. "Best get you back and hosed down or your mam will go nuts with me." He pulls on her hood playfully and she slightly falls back laughing. "I loved every minute of last night, and I think I would like to stay a little smelly for a while longer." Although her head is heavy; her heart is full, and she doesn't want this moment to end.

She never thought for a moment that this would top anything in her life so far. Two years ago, all she thought of was going out with her mates, having her hair done with a full face of make-up. Now she is standing in freezing in a field with sheep birth plastered to her face, and she couldn't be happier. "I think we start like sheep, some of us," she says, scratching her nose and then tugging on Ed's arm so he'll listen to her. "You know, we follow as we're not sure of ourselves at first, until one day it's like we start to see ourselves a little more clearly, then we're free to create our own path."

Ed stops and looks down at her. "I have always known you're not a sheep, Eva. Even when I use to chase you with dried shit on a stick when we were eight," he tickles her neck, and she squirms away from him.

"I will shove that shit down your throat if you're not careful," she replies, reaching up on her tiptoes to kiss him.

"Do you think your parents would take me on as an apprentice? I'm sure I could go to college part time or change my degree," she asks, as serious as Eva has ever been. "I will ask, but I don't think your Dad's going to take that well, not his little princess on a farm." Ed is only speaking the truth. She puts her head down. "He's too focused on himself right now, like Mum, to probably notice."

"Let's get them wobbly bits of yours washed down," he grabs her bum, and they play fight onto the car park. "Can I stay here a bit longer?" she pleads with him.

"As much as I would like that, me ma doesn't want old Martha to bury her in the old veg plot with the rest for keeping you here all night."

He opens the car door and Eva sits on the bin bag lining the seats. She pauses to register what Ed has said. "What do you mean, old veg patch with the rest?" She crosses her arms and refuses to put her seat belt on until he answers. "Just a slip of the tongue. Come on. You know people here are slightly fearful of your Gran and your family."

Eva wasn't having any of it. "No, she's strange and harsh at times, yes, but she's just Gran," she says defensively. "What exactly do you mean? Tell me?"

"Okay" Ed rubs his forehead as he knows this is going to land him in the shit. "So, your Grandad died and there was no open-top coffin? The funeral wasn't advertised locally, so only a few mourners turned up. Gossip circulated that she killed him off and buried him in the garden." Ed wishes he had kept his trap shut.

"Grandad wanted a closed coffin and a low-key funeral that's all. You gossip about everyone," she says, hurt and annoyed. Why would he say such a thing. "Eva, please don't, you must have heard some kind of gossip before?" Has she been living in a parallel universe, he wonders? Who doesn't know her family play dirty? "Please don't fall out with me," he starts the engine, annoyed. "Fuck's sake." He hits reverse and pulls the Defender out of the farm driveway.

Eva refuses to look at him as the car pulls up at her Mums. Ed stops the car and gets out. He goes round to Eva's side and swings the door open. He leans into her and kisses her pouted lips. "People say shit, but last night it was you and me against the world. I want that, nothing less." Eva slides down from the seat and lands before him.

"Even when I smell like a year's worth of sweat?" she starts to calm down. "Together in sweat," he nibbles on her nose as they both put their arms in the air and clasp hands. He pushes her slightly into the side of the seat and tickles her again until she can't stop laughing.

Eva slowly walks across the gravel to the front door, turning back and waving to Ed as he gets in the car. She sits on the porch, pulls her sleeves over her hands and watches as he drives off into the misty rain, reminiscing about last night. Looking back towards the front door, she remembers how it used to feel like the safest place in the world. Now it just seems like a miserable building - a place people go to for unhappiness. The only good thing is her dog, Alex. She figures maybe it's time to move out.

A car appears at the gates and thinking it's Ed coming back, she gets up, hoping he's changed his mind and she can go back to the farm with him, but it's not his car. A bright red Ford Focus stops at the gates, and it seems to be a taxi. The driver waves at her to confirm he's there. Eva waves back and feeling confused she walks over to tell him he has the wrong house, but the front door suddenly opens. A well-dressed man appears on the porch, and he's trying to close the door gently behind him but struggles to get it to close firmly. He sees Eva glaring and covered in sheep birth and jumps out of his skin. "Sneaking off, are you?" she says, almost as if it's a telling off. The taxi driver flashes his head lights, and the man puts his thumb up and smiles nervously. "Do you not talk?" Eva continues. "You're sneaking out my home early in the morning and you have nothing to say?"

He looks baffled. "I am sorry, and you are?" The man looks at her and then towards the taxi, cornered and startled. She walks a little closer to him. "Eva, and I live here. Shall I call the police?" She pretends to dial a number on her phone. "No need Miss. I am Harsmit, a friend of your Mums. I didn't want to wake her." He then reasserts himself, stands up tall and is suddenly very business-like. Eva puts the phone in her hoodie pouch. "Go then." Eva gestures towards the taxi with its engine running. Harsmit puts both hands up as a thank you and walks speedily towards the gate, not looking back. The rain gets heavier, and he struggles up the mount towards the taxi whose driver is getting impatient.

E va puts her hood up and watches as he goes off in the taxi. Feeling vengeful, she texts her Dad.

'Hi Dad, just confirming I got home safe a day ago all good up here, and as you had been enquiring about Mum's health recently, I can confirm to you that she is well and currently dating again. Love E x.'

She slams the front door as she enters the house. "I hope she heard that," Eva mutters to herself. Stripping her clothes off she leaves them at the front door and heads for the guest room shower. She slams about in the bathroom hoping to wake her Mum, but no noise comes from the upstairs. The house is silent.

Chapter Twenty

THE PAISLEY

The first-class coach from London to Halifax is empty. Dylan looks down the aisle to the other coaches, which seem to be jam-packed with people. Although he enjoys the quiet and can afford this perk, he could do with a distraction from his thoughts. The connections to London from Halifax are now regular and for most services, it's just short of three hours, but the prices are steep unless you book early. It's a luxury only for those who can afford it.

His head is fogged with Claire's confession. He can't remember because it didn't happen. All because Richard, for some reason, believed he could manipulate his Mum. But why was he so obsessed with her? It was he and Hannah whose lives were blown apart by all his trickery. A sinking feeling hits him, to know the truth settles him, but understanding why unnerves him. He never believed he could have cheated on Hannah. The not remembering part has tortured him. Now it's clear to him how far people will go for personal gain.

He sits reading his phone, it's not an e-book but the text from Eva he received early this morning. He had hoped to return to break the news and in the hope that Hannah would suddenly just forgive him, but how could she? He couldn't forgive or forget the betrayal that had also been done to him. He reads the message repeatedly. Hannah hasn't moved on; these men are just stop gaps that she's using to replace what they had together. He must believe this. They had a strong marriage, and many challenges had come their way, but adultery was the final straw in the partnership. He's sure he can convince her to believe him and start again, no more running away. Her reaction at Maggie's funeral proves this. She seemed completely devastated at Mum's speech, so there's still strong feelings and the fact that they have slept together since the split, which may have made her pregnant. Is she still pregnant? Why has she still said nothing to him about it? Is it this other bloke? The pain caused has been so much, maybe she can't bring herself to tell him. So many questions he must ask. This new man can't possibly be the father. The timings don't match.

The train arrives at Halifax. Dylan gets off and prepares to sort out a taxi to go straight to see Hannah, but to his surprise Martha is standing outside the station leaning against her Range Rover waiting for him. She beams as he walks out of the station. "As soon as you said you had hopped on the morning train; I thought I would come down and meet you." Martha moves in for a hug. Dylan responds but cautiously. She never meets him. However, the last time he saw her, they fought over her funeral speech so she must feel bad and is trying to make it up to him. "Do you want me to drive?" he asks.

"Yes, my sciatica's playing up." Martha walks around to the passenger side and they both get in.

They headed off to Martha's farm, 'The Paisley,' which is in the heart of the valley and used as a horse-riding school, stabling and dog boarding facility. Martha has always loved horses since she was little and in recent years took on dog boarding for locals, and a small extra business grew from this. The area is deserted, and quiet and so neighbours don't complain about the noise, in fact, most of them are regular clients. Dylan tries hard to hide his feelings at having to change his plans, but he's itching to get over to see Hannah and Eva. But

Martha seems intent on distracting him with issues around the farm, determined not to let him wriggle free. So far, she has taken him around it like a tourist pointing out the renovations required to extend the boarding kennels and exercise area for the horses, and she's now blathering on about the horse box at the Shibden where local riders are now stopping along the bridle path to have a quick coffee and a breakfast roll.

Finally, he can take it no longer. "Mum, I need to go see Hannah, it's important," he puts his foot down, stopping her in her tracks. "I have news, which could change everything and try and bring what we had back to the way it was," he says. Martha shows no reaction to this. "Nothing in life can ever be what it was, Dylan and that is a fact!" Wow, he thinks, she's being very cold with him. He never understood why she's so uncaring at times. "Mum, do you not want me to be happy? She makes me happy and always has. My information will change so much and clarify a few things". He's wondering why she's not listening to him.

Martha turns her back to him and leans against her stick. "What information, given the situation, could possibly make anything better, Dylan?" He walks around to face her, and she tries to look away.

"I have met with Claire down in Kent." Martha's eyes widen, and she now looks more interested. "She said it was all a lie that Richard framed me, and nothing ever happened between us. She said that they wanted to blackmail you, but for some reason Hannah got the pictures instead of you." He pleads with her to believe him. Martha tuts loudly. "You can't believe a word that little druggy says. Did you record it?" Why didn't he think to do that? "No." Dylan knows he's missed a trick here and sighs knowing he was an idiot.

"Well, in that case you have nothing!" Martha is being harsh, but she's right. Dylan puts his hands to his face in despair. He wasn't thinking properly. "She not answering my calls. I never thought about it like that." He didn't want anyone to know they had met originally so it never crossed his mind. "You're a god-damn lawyer, Dylan. You should know to get proof!" Martha puts her hand on his shoulder to comfort him, but he shrugs it off, annoyed with himself. "Why are you punishing yourself like this? It's all done now. The only way is to move forward. You will find another more well-suited partner," she says this in a know-it-all way.

"I don't want another. I want Hannah and I believe Claire, as Richard was a fucking tool. He was always messing about trying to trip people up. In fact, he was your little bitch for a time, wasn't he?" he points at her. She pushes his finger down. "Don't you dare speak to me that way." Martha then slaps his legs with her stick and begins to hit him as he backs off down the back garden path. Dylan jumps out of her way. "Mum, what the hell are you doing?" he cowers.

Rustling can be heard from someone riding their horse making their way through the garden below towards the stable. Martha stops and asserts herself, afraid they're being watched. "I won't take no shit from any man, Dylan. Be it you or your father before you. You have made your bed and you need to lie it and take control."

Dylan suddenly feels a fear he's forgotten about. It's like he is a little kid again. He looks at her full of sorrow, "Sorry Mum, it's all been too much, and I just wanted a happy life like you and Dad." Martha smiles at him. "No, I am sorry. I get protective over our family and business. Sometimes I get a like a bulldog and forget you are my flesh and blood. My only baby." He offers her his arm to help her back to the house, and she takes it smiling like the cat that has got the cream.

"I am glad you are back. We have important business matters to discuss," she taps his hand as they walk past the rose garden. "We have unwanted interest in the business from a Bradford based group. They are undercutting a lot of our bids," she explains. "But we have the name and quality to prove our good work." Dylan is unaware of this, as nothing has been discussed in London. "Times change and people are looking to save a few pounds," she continues, "this group is aware of this and are spreading their wings across Halifax and Huddersfield. We have contracts set up with the Business Council, but they are out to tender, so it's important we pull together and show a united front." Martha stops to smell the roses that are starting to bloom. "I refuse, even at my age, to lay down and let this business that has topped this area for several years, die." She inhales the roses scent.

"It's not dying Mum, Dad built it strong." Dylan reminds her. If looks could kill, Dylan would be a goner. "I built it with him. No man is ever alone. He may have been the face, but I was the backbone and don't you forget that."

Dylan looks towards the old pond that his Dad never finished. Martha never touched it after he died. It was a personal project. "So, this nonsense with Claire needs to be put to the side and business is now the focus. Besides, Hannah has her own little projects and seemingly loving the single life, so let her go Dylan and concentrate on yourself for once." Martha goes into the kitchen and pops the kettle on. Dylan is still staring at the pond and Martha brings him a brew. "I just didn't have the heart to touch it and now look at it." Dylan sips the tea.

"It's a mess, all overgrown." Martha leans her head on him.

"Yes, all overgrown and finding its own path. It's making its own choices and reclaiming itself just as nature should. Perhaps you should take comfort in that."

Chapter Twenty-One

GIN & GOSSIP

Ruth is sitting alone pushing a straw around her glass of Elderflower and water while watching the ice cubes crash against each other. Now and again blowing bubbles into the glass. Resting her elbows on the table, she's getting restless waiting for Hannah to arrive. The sirloin and rocket sourdough pizza smell is driving her tastebuds wild, and she's tempted to eat one before Hannah arrives. The outdoor pizzas are a solid staple of a classic Shibden summer. You know spring is in full flow and summer is on its way when the grill fires up.

She looks around the beer garden with its wide rustic wooden chairs allowing the evening sun to melt into her skin and then notices the bees pollinating the flower baskets surrounding the gleaming white mill building. You could be tricked into believing you're in the middle of The Dales not a five-minute drive from Halifax town centre. It's a little diamond nestled perfectly in valley belly.

"Have you ordered?" Hannah sits down. She's a little giddier than usual. "You look annoyingly happy." Ruth is very sharp.

"A little mean, don't you think, Ruth?" Hannah shrugs it off.

"I'm just hungry. I've been sitting here for fifteen minutes. Considering you could basically just roll down the hill and land on this bench from yours."

"I've been dealing with Eva. Again." Hannah huffs. "I support her decision to leave Uni, but now she wants to be a farm hand and go to college." She browses the menu and orders a drink. "I don't disagree, but I just don't want to think it's because of a boy." Ruth looks up, thinking the apple doesn't fall far from the tree. "And look how that turned out for you!" Hannah is used to the sarky comments and figured Ruth must be on her period.

"God, Ruth, did you get out of the wrong side of bed this morning?" Putting the menu to the side, she gestures to the waiter to place an order. "Beetroot, rocket and goat's cheese for me," Hannah orders and then looks at Ruth. "Sirloin, please," Ruth says through gritted teeth as her belly rumbles.

"So Harsmit is not who I thought he was. To be honest, it's a pleasant surprise and refreshing." She has a warm expression on her face, and this seems to make Ruth feel worse. "Oh, straight to you. Did you ever think I had something to say for once or do I just sit here waiting for the Halifax Hannah to turn up and life begins?" Ruth can't stop herself from snapping at Hannah. She tries to control herself but it's difficult. These hormones are wild.

Hannah refuses to engage, she sees Ruth wants an argument. "Okay then, what is so important that you are having a meltdown with me, and to be honest, being a bitch!" Hannah leans into prompt Ruth to speak. Ruth goes to confess why she's feeling irate, she so wants to tell her friend, but fear takes over and she can't seem to let the words come out of her mouth. "Nothing, I'm just crabby as I still can't locate Zofia. I shouldn't have snapped. I do like to see you happy, maybe I'm just a little jealous and clearly, he's pushing the right buttons." Ruth just can't own up.

The pizzas arrive and Ruth tucks in. She waves to a small group of women staring at them across the garden. "However, those women over there keep staring at you. Do you know them?" Ruth stares back again so they notice her watching and they turn back to the table. Hannah shrugs "It's some of the mums from the horse-riding school at Martha's. As you can tell, they hate me. The one with the bad highlights had a thing for Dylan when I used to take Eva riding there. Had no problem flirting with him constantly in front of me." Hannah bites into her pizza. "I wonder if he ever had sex with any of them. Probably why they're talking. Probably thinking I should've known what he was like all along." Ruth finishes her Elderflower and makes a loud sucking noise with the straw. She turns towards them. "Well, they should be thinking if your husband can cheat what's theirs up to when they are not around." She says this loudly, so they hear.

Hannah stands up and goes towards the toilet, and on her way, she passes the table. One of the women gives her a wave and shouts, "Hi."

Hannah politely says "hi" back with a false smile. She just about manages to get to the toilet door without having to make conversation with them. But Mandy Mills from the group stops her. The woman with the bad highlights. "So sorry to hear about your breakup." She's not sorry, she's loving every minute of her pain. "Dylan was such a catch. It must have been hard for you to keep him all these years. At least you can now relax." Mandy sticks her modified chest out like a peacock. Hannah doesn't bite, instead she musters up a sad face and suggests "You know, Mandy, Dylan had a fetish for horses, you might want to check yours at the farm, after all everyone is always happy with Martha's services."

Mandy goes to answer back but is interrupted by some of the local old boys, who grabs Hannah and gives her a big hug. "I tell yah, Mandy, didn't I tell you this one is much better off without a money grabbing Burnside. Always said she was too good for him." Keith Ball is a little worse for wear but at least he's speaking more sense than Mandy. Mandy takes the defeat and goes back to her table. "Come drink with us, Miss ex-Burnside?" Keith has done most of the electrics at Hannah's house, but she's not his drinking buddy. "Another time." She heads to the loo.

Ruth watches the commotion but decides Hannah can handle herself with that lot. After all, her pizza needs polishing off. She then orders a cheeseboard because, for some reason, cheese seems to be her comfort food now. But she suddenly feels sick again, and Hannah is in the mood to chat all night. Ruth just feels the need to get home and lie down. Hannah sits back down. Ruth knocks Hannah's drink and plate off the table and sways like she's had too much to drink. "How much vodka and Elderflowers have you had tonight?" Hannah picks up the glass and plate. People stop to watch, and Preston comes over to help clear the table. "Hannah Banana, I am a wee bit pished, take me home, please?" Ruth does her puppy-dog eyes. Hannah is used to Ruth having one too many. Others might say it's because she's Scottish, but Hannah and Ruth know it's because she's just a lightweight.

Ruth is hopeful this performance will get her out of having to have a long unwanted conversation about Hannah's date and about Ruth's current health. Hannah is a little peeved off. "Okay, I'll go in and sort the bill, try to stay in an upright position," she says and goes to the indoor bar to settle the bill. Preston, the duty manger, hands her the bill and she notices only two Elderflower and sodas. It can't be right. Ruth is sure to have had at least three vodkas before Hannah arrived. "Is that correct? Are you sure we don't have another tab?" she enquires. Preston goes over and checks the till. "Nope love, that's all that's there. I gave Ruth the drink myself, was surprised she didn't have vodka."

Hannah looks out at Ruth, who is suddenly not swaying but sat talking on her phone. The machine beeps as the card clears and Preston hands her a receipt. "Nice to see you can all still visit after everything that has happened. I was just saying the same to Dylan today." Hannah puts the receipt in her bag, he must be mistaken. "Dylan's in London."

she says unsure why Preston would think he was here. "No, he was here for a lunch meeting with some friends this afternoon." Poor Preston wishes he hadn't put his foot in it. Hannah sees he looks uncomfortable. "None of my business anymore, thank you for the lovely meal." She walks out to assess the Ruth situation, but her seat is empty.

Ruth has made her way to the car park just as a taxi pulls in. She walks around swiftly to the passenger side and gets in. "I didn't want to put you out, so I called a taxi. Thank you for paying, it's on me next time." She then opens the car door, thinking she needs to move fast. "And you're only up the hill, I know you like to walk so get them steps in," she shuts the taxi door, and it drives off leaving Hannah standing in the car park watching it leave. Her phone rings and it's Harsmit. "Hello, Sleeping Beauty, how's you?" That put a beaming smile back on her face.

"Oh, I've had better days." The signal goes as she is too low in the valley. Great! Abandoned by your mate in the car park and then lost in connection with your chat date, what a way to end an evening.

Chapter Twenty-Two

MAGGIE'S BOOKS

The stuffy little sitting room lays quiet and untouched, it's almost like Maggie is about to come through the door and sit down to read her new book by the fire with a Martini in her hand. The house has sat empty since her passing and only the light from the windows stretches across bookshelves that vastly surround the living area. Martha sits on Maggie's high-back chair next to the log fire which still has ash from its last light spilling on to the wool rug beneath it.

Rubbing her fingers up and down the cold leather arms of the chair, she rests her weary head back against the cotton head rest Maggie had sewn. Martha warms her cheeks on the soft fabric and slowly inhales the smell that was once Maggie's. It's still slightly there but the fabric is cold and damp as the room has been lifeless. Surround by a world of stories, Martha can only think of the one that was hers and Maggie's. A tale she plans never to tell and like Maggie, she will take to her grave.

Putting her hand in her inside pocket, she takes out her glasses pouch, shakes her small, rimmed specs on her knees then gently places them on her face, pushing them up so they snuggly sit on her nose. "Oh, what a friend you had been," Martha talks aloud as if Maggie was there. She gazes around the room, looking for an answer. "To think of all these books you have read. Did you really read them? I suppose you being you, yes you did," she mocks Maggie's voice. "Nowt good on telly.

Yah can always count on a book." Laughing at her friend's memories, she struggles a little to push herself forward in the chair. "Let's see what you got here." Leaning on her stick and pulling herself up right, she stands dead centre in the small entrance room of Maggie's end terrace.

A slow half turn brings Martha back round to face the fireplace. A picture of her and Maggie as little children sitting on the hill overlooking Halifax takes pride of place on the shelf. Picking it up Martha reminisces and pulls the picture to her face and gently kisses it. Noticing the picture next to it, her expression changes and her rage unleashes as she grabs it and aggressively smashes it against the fireplace until the glass makes a loud noise, shattering onto the unlit fire logs.

Pulling the photo out from the broken glass she holds it up into the light. Her husband's face stares back at her. He has his arms around Richard and Dylan. They look so young, just babies. Martha and Maggie are standing at either side of Jock smiling. "Hm, happy little family," she mutters. She tears it in half, keeping the side with her and Dylan in it. She then looks again at the other half before tossing it into the fireplace. Martha takes the matches from the shelf, lights one, and throws it on top of the picture. She closes her eyes in pain as the picture of Jock, Maggie, and Richard melts away in front of her. Gripping the fire surround, she screams loudly.

Her breathing is becoming erratic, and she steadies herself. Sniffing loudly and inhaling a large gulp of air, she swings her stick around the room and shouts, "Where is it? I know you had it! You crafty little minx. That piece of shit son of yours must have sent it to you." Her stick hits a table lamp which crashes onto the rug below. In a frantic rage Martha then pulls all the books off the shelves looking for what she thinks Maggie may have had. Book after book tumble onto the floor and Martha tries to steady her balance and climb over to the next bookshelf, slipping on books as she goes.

All the shelves are now clear, and the books are spread across the floor of the tiny room. You can't even see the floor anymore. Martha sits in the middle of the room surround by the mess she has just made. She looks like a little bird perched in a book nest. Biting on her bottom lip she screams into herself and rocks back and forth with frustration. "I am in control. I am in control!" She repeats continuously to herself and holds back tears that are desperate to break through. Some pills of Maggie's are sitting on the side table next to the Oxblood chairs. Martha crawls towards the table and with a struggle, pulls herself up. Opening the bottle and not caring what's inside of it she throws two pills into her mouth, pushes them around her mouth and then swallows quickly.

A van can be heard outside and, it's trying to get into the street, but some of the terraces on the hill only have small roads outside them. Martha can hear a loud voice telling the drivers how to do a three-point turn in the enclosed space. It must be the removal men. She supposes Dangerous Dug is good for something. They are already twenty minutes late. Kicking the books out of her way she clears a path to the front door with her stick. They have finally managed to turn the van around, however, they have also just blocked the entire lane and left the van just sat there in the middle of the road. Dug and Jamie come towards Martha, one carrying his phone and the younger one struggling with the packing boxes and tape.

"You alright, love?" Dangerous Dug says, rubbing his hands as he reaches Martha. "You're late!" she stamps her stick. He looks a little taken aback. "Yeah, traffic is shagged." He then looks behind Martha at the terrace. "Any chance of a brew?"

"The electric's off," she hisses at him. "I don't pay for brews and as you charge an hourly rate, I will be deducting this time off the bill," she looks down at her watch. The poor bloke feels put in his place. He looks round at the younger one who has now dropped most of the packing boxes all over the small grassy path leading to the door.

"Get yourself in there lad, sharpish," he tries to impress Martha, but she's not interested.

She extends her hand out and produces the house keys. "You have your allotted time. I expect every single item in that house listed and boxed up, nothing is left behind. I repeat nothing!" She looks at him for an answer. He stumbles a little. "Yes, of course, love." She gives him a look of disapproval. She drops the keys into his dry, dirty hands. "Once complete, move to the unit. Max will be there. The address is in the email I sent to you, then return the keys to the Burnside building in Halifax town centre." The younger lad's eyes suddenly light up and he looks at Martha like she's the prize at the local fayre.

"Burnside?" he gasps.

"Yes, Burnside," she confirms slowly and clearly.

"Your wish is my command," replies Dug, and he tosses the keys in the air, shoving the other fella into the house.

Martha shakes her head in disgust, at least they've managed not to block her car. The curtains of the house next door twitch slightly. "Here we go, the local Shibden grapevine, watching my every move." Sliding past the oversized, badly parked van she heads to her Range Rover parked down the lane where she expected the packers to park. It takes her more time these days to climb in and out, but she pulls herself up onto the driver's seat. Searching her pockets for her phone, she finds it and dials the warehouse unit.

A weary voice answers. "Yo, Mrs Burnside." Why is everyone so bloody lazy these days? She thinks. "Stop answering like an American rapper! The packers are here. Better late than never. I want the boxes to be put in room order and once opened tomorrow, every item catalogued. Nothing can be missed, do you understand Max?" No answer comes back, just silence. She shouts, "Max do you understand? Answer me." Max is too busy playing on his PlayStation and hasn't been listening to anything. "Max," she shouts again. He nearly drops the phone. "Yes, I got it sorry, just making a coffee." Martha's trying to remain calm. The only good thing about Max is that he notices nothing, that's why she uses him. "It's also Dangerous Dug doing the moving, so make sure the CCTV is on." She then hangs up on him. "Idiot," she mumbles to herself.

Adjusting the rear-view mirror, she looks back at Maggie's home. The clouds are a little grey behind it and no sun is coming through. "You'll do as a rental," she smirks to herself and drives out to the main road, swerving around the potholes as she goes.

Chapter Twenty-Three

THE WATER PEOPLE

The Private water company has had their roadworks outside the shop and it has been causing problems for weeks now. More than three times, the cobbled road has been closed for maintenance. You would think they had fixed the problem by now. Ruth has taken it upon herself to have strict words with the poor people who are, after all, just doing their job. They see her making her way up the street and since this is not her first visit, they put on their noise cancelling headphones and start digging. She shouts at them, but they gesture that they can't hear, and she storms back into the shop nearly taking the hinges off the door as she goes.

She glares at them through the glass. "Why couldn't they fix the problem the first-time round?" She shouts at the front window and making faces at them. They just smile politely back. Hannah thinks they enjoy winding Ruth up. She's not interested in the roadworks, she's too busy texting Harsmit to notice. Ruth sticks her middle finger up at them. "We have two large deliveries today and you know how funny Arron gets not being able to park near." He's a strange one. Ruth has known him for years and can't read him properly. Never seems to have any money and can't keep a job.

Noticing Hannah is smiling at her phone and not listening to anything, she shouts, "Oi, Martha's here to buy her second batch of lady oil!" she says right in front of Hannah's face. Hannah looks up from her phone. "What?" She replies with a confused look.

"You're bloody listening now, aren't you?" Ruth hits a whip on the glass counter. Hannah puts her phone away. "I'm sorry, it's just he wants to go for a walk. When does a bloke want to go for a walk?" Hitting the whip again, Ruth replies, "All the time. They have three legs but prefer the middle one," and mimics a hand gesture in front of her mouth.

"Shut up, Ruth" Hannah scowls. "I haven't even seen the middle one yet, it's not got that far." She seems a little put out by that. Taking it slow is fine, but not one sexual advance so far. She's starting to feel a little dehydrated below. Ruth relishes this information. "What do you think he wants then, Han? World fuckin' peace?" Ruth now slaps the whip on her hand. "It's what they all want. Don't let them kid you with this modern man shite."

"It's not always about sex." Hannah hates it when Ruth is always so anti men. Ruth slides her bum across Hannah's leg.

"What did you feel?" she asks.

"Violated." Hannah answers.

"Yes, as a female, but with a bloke it would be an instant crotch volcano! All the same, every last one, probably got its own little brain in the ball sack." She then leans against the counter. "Thought by now you would have at least realised that's a given." Hannah slams her hand next to Ruth. "Given what? That my husband couldn't keep it in his expensive pants!" Ruth folds her arms and asserts herself.

"Well, yes that, but I was just talking about age." Hannah screams out loud. "What's age got to do with it?" Hannah knows she can't win this conversation. Ruth decides to back off. "We just get more perspective with age, that's all I meant."

Ｔhe bell rings and Hannah and Ruth turn to look at the door at the same time. Harsmit is standing in the doorway wearing a grey t-shirt and jeans and he's holding a box of donuts. Ruth doesn't get the attraction. He looks, well, so clean. But anyone willing to bribe her with food deserves a chance. "Okay, he gets my vote. Donuts win every time," Ruth whispers to Hannah. Harsmit looks uneasy as she approaches and grabs the donuts from him. "Afternoon ladies, yes, help yourselves," he says as he tries without success to keep a hold of the donuts from Ruth.

Hannah quickly checks her reflection in the cabinet as she wasn't expecting him to be here so soon and also to be so casually dressed. She liked the whole dinner jacket look he had going. "You're early. I thought we were meeting at the park?" Harsmit starts looking around the shop. "I thought I would check out the infamous 'Pleasure Not Sin' for myself," he continues looking around. Ruth, with a mouth full of jam donut, says, "Oh, so you have heard of us. Would sir like to go to the changing room, and we can bring over this week's specials of cock rings?" Harsmit is not quite sure if she's serious, so he laughs it off.

"No, quite happy just to browse." Ruth does a big fake smile.

"Suit yourself," and she sits back, licking the jam off her fingers.

Hannah gives her a dirty look, aware Ruth is only being protective in her own way, but bloody willy rings, really? So, she gives Harsmit a tour. "Ignore the human dust bin over there," she says, putting her hand up and waving them about like an airhostess. "It's only small as we have a unit for mass stock, so this ickle shop floor is just a few tantalising treasures for local browsers." He puts his hands in his pockets.

"So, you don't get much footfall?" He seems genuinely interested.

"No, the odd regular and kids having a laugh most days as most is done online, but we have a large customer base now. Sex sells!" His face goes a little red and Hannah starts to feel a little stupid, but Ruth intervenes. "You should see my vag table. It's a collector's item." She nods at him confidently.

Hannah isn't letting this embarrassment go on any further. "Let's get out of here. Is your car on the next street?" She throws Ruth more daggers, but Ruth is too busy demolishing her third donut. Harsmit just nods. He too would like to make a sharp exit. Ruth waves them off, donut in hand, but is glad they have gone because now the real work needs to start.

She is determined to sort the road issue out. She notices that the workmen have now left the top of the street for the day, and it still says 'Road Closed'. She cleans her jammy fingers on some wipes and sets off to the top of the street to, yet again, assess the situation Ruth-style. They have dug a large hole and put barriers up to stop anyone falling in and there seem to be too many barriers. It looks like a van could fit down the street at a push. Deciding that there's room, Ruth moves two of the barriers, closing the street off, and then pushes the road closed sign a little further down so you can only just see it. She brushes the dirt off her hands and does a walk of victory as she proudly makes her way back to the shop. The girls in the hairdressers next door give her a little cheer, as this seems to have been the bane of the whole street and she takes a bow like a true champ of the people celebrating with the masses.

Searching through the mound of invoices for the deliveries she's expecting for the week, she finds today's scheduled delivery numbers and starts to dial from the shop's landline. This is a particular favourite, as it's a bright pink set of boobs in shiny plastic, a little something she picked up in Germany a few years ago while on a trip with Zofia. It's amazing what you find in second hand shops and that was their thing, her and Zofia browsing little shops on city breaks throughout the year, sitting in little cafes in the day then going to crazy raves in the evening, dressing up and being their mad selves.

Picking up the phone to dial the delivery driver's number, she decides to put on the voice of Audrey Hepburn. "Is that the one and only Arron, delivery man to the stars?" The reception is a little crackly as the phone is very dated. "Yeah, who's this? I don't have any money. So don't even ask!" He's very straight forward and defensive.

"It's Ruth, you idiot from Pleasure Not Sin, not a debt chaser. The road is no longer closed, and you should be able to squeeze the van through. Any problems, just call me back on this number," she sounds so proud of herself, like she had just parted the Red Sea. "Excellent mate, traffic is good, and we are running on time so expect to see yah around 5pm. Could I borrow £20?" Ruth places the phone down in its double D bra shaped holder. She looks in the till, but it's empty, so he's out of luck.

Resting both hands on the counter, she smiles at herself in the reflection on the counter, given that life at present feels to be a little against her. You've got to take the wins no matter how small they are. "That's a win for Ruth and nil to the fucking Business Council," she declares out loud believing them to be causing the delays on purpose. With that, she decides to celebrate because one last sugar-coated donut won't hurt.

Chapter Twenty-Four

MR WELL DRESSED

E d and Eva are driving through the town centre on the way back to the farm. They have the windows down and listening to Paolo Nutini on full blast. Eva loves him and is determined to sway Ed, who's not so keen. But he's letting her have the car karaoke moment of her life. Her hands are out of the open window feeling the fast-moving air between her fingertips as she belts her little heart out. Ed's trying to drive but keeps looking at her, she seems herself again and he now has everything he ever wanted. He's longed for Eva for as long as he can remember, and he's not letting her go.

Ed glimpses a Bentley as they pass through town. "Ev, is that your mam getting in that Bentley? Man, that woman has good taste." Eva slumps back in the chair. Ed and his love of cars, she thinks.

"Mr 'Well-Dressed'?"

"Never mind his clothes, the car is ace." Ed can't hide his excitement from Eva. He follows the Bentley out of the town centre.

"Why are you following them?" Eva is now a little pissed off at his childish behaviour and is huffing in the passenger seat. "We are going their way," he casually says, but notably speeds up. The Bentley turns into Shibden Park and Ed and Eva continue onto the farm.

The car pulls into the lower car park of Shibden Park. Hannah gets out and breathes in the fresh air, glad to be away from the shop. It's not too busy today even though the weather is calm and not raining for once. Harsmit gestures over towards the café. "Fancy an ice cream as we walk along?" He rubs his belly like a naughty child. Hannah's not a big ice cream fan. "I'd prefer a nice warm cup of tea."

They place their order and wait outside on the picnic benches outside the café. From there you get to look up at the great hall as it dominates high over the lower level surrounding of the park. "You ever been in?" Hannah asks him. She smiles at him and her hair glints in the sunshine. Harsmit doesn't take his eyes off her. "Maybe once when I was a boy, but I don't really remember it. Not been over this way in years. Dad goes on about it all the time, but I've always been well, too busy." A lad shouts out their order and Hannah picks it up, putting extra milk in her tea to cool it down.

Harsmit put his hand out, she takes it, and he leads them off toward the boating pond. Hannah tries to shake off the earlier conversation with Ruth about men and three legs. Well, this is a very public spot, so for once Ruth is wrong. He licks the bottom of his cone as the ice cream drips down onto his other hand. "Your husband's family seems to be well known round here?" he gently asks. Oh, why does he need to bring bloody Dylan up?

"Well, they have lived in these parts for years. His Dad was from Scotland and his Mum lived up that hill," she points to the other side of the valley."

"Oh, so she's the Yorkshire lass, and he's the Scot, made a lot of money and..." Hannah interrupts as she doesn't like the line of questioning. "Can we not talk about them?" She doesn't understand why he's asking about the Burnsides suddenly.

She tries to turn the conversation around. "I would like to know more about you, since we are still chat buddies," she half-heartedly laughs. Harsmit looks a little wary, he didn't mean to overstep. "Sorry, I sometime ask too many questions, it's just that they all seemed to know you at the café."

"They don't know me at all." Hannah puts her head down. "Just a vision of what the family wants them to see. I've tried to stay away from the business side since last year." She looks out at the boats. Little memories of her and Dylan messing around when they first got together on the little boats come back to her. He was fun back then.

Harsmit put ice cream on her nose, and she comes back to reality. "You're a little day dreamer, aren't you?" She feels like she has just been caught out. She wipes off the ice cream on her sleeve. He points to her bag. "Your phone keeps buzzing, do you need to get it?" She taps on her bag and says,

"Nope." She then reaches for his hand, and they walk up towards the big house on the hill.

Sitting in the shadow of the Great Hall, they watch people go by, families with little kids, walkers, and history tours of the building. "Can see why my Dad likes it here. Tell him he doesn't need to drive no more, but he loves it. Or so he says. I think he likes to hide from me Mum," he laughs at himself. "So much history and the view not too bad either," he winks at Hannah. She gives him a playful nudge back. "So, are we still on a chatting friend basis or is there some kind of friends scale we creep up to?" At this point he puts his arm round Hannah's shoulders. She doesn't seem reluctant to move it and slowly leans over and settles herself next to him. "Not really thought that far, I mean there's not a chatty scale to properly follow," she smirks at him. Looking out and finishing her now very cold tea, she takes a deep breath. "Let's take it slow, not snail slow, but just see how it goes." Harsmit kisses the end of her nose with his honey lips that she loves. "So, Halifax Hannah does this mean we are now snail mates," and tickles her.

"No, we are officially dating." Hannah tries not to smile.

"Look at you trying not to look cute," Harsmit laughs at her, trying to hide her feelings. "On a very honest note, there's something I have been meaning to say since we sat down." He looks deadly serious. Hannah becomes a little alarmed. What is he going to say? She thought it was going well so far. Harsmit slaps his head. "Why didn't you tell me my car needed a wash? Look at it from here?" Hannah slaps his knee.

"You vain idiot. Men and their bloody love of cars."

Hannah looks down at the car park as the sun reflects off the Bentley. "Yeah, it looks pretty shit, mate," she laughs. Harsmit pretends to be offended and falls over like she has hit him in the heart. He gets his phone out. "Come on, let's get dirty." Oh god, Hannah thinks, the man with three legs. He sees her shock reaction. "A dirty car selfie, silly." They both lean and make funny faces as the car sits in the distance. "You make me laugh and I need that, but I best get back. Ruth's been pretty unwell at the moment." Hannah looks in her bag.

"Is it serious?" he asks. Hannah stops and thinks, is it serious? Ruth hasn't been herself for the last month. "Err, I am sure it's nothing," but she's not sure, to be honest.

Taking her phone from her bag, she notices several missed calls from Ruth. She listens to her voice mail. Ruth is frantic, saying there's been an accident outside the shop. "We need to go now. Something has happened at the shop." Hannah panics. Harsmit grabs both of her hands. "Okay, calm down, I will get you there in no time."

They both run down the grassy hill towards the car park and get into the car. Hannah texts Ruth that she will be there ASAP. "What an end to a date. Whatever it is, we will deal with it so please try not to worry." Harsmit is trying his best to give Hannah some kind of comfort. It's not working as she is frantically fidgeting with her nails in the front seat. Ruth seems really panicked, and she's been ill for too long. The road is full of traffic into Halifax. "Come on traffic," Hannah shouts. "It always queues from Stump Cross for no fucking reason," and she hits the dashboard.

"Swearing is not going to help. It's moving, and we will be there soon." Harsmit seems really calm, but Hannah has an uneasy feeling in her gut and she's learning quickly to trust it. As they finally get nearer to where the street the shop is on, the traffic has now come to a standstill as the police divert the cars past the street entrance. Hannah's heart is thumping in her chest, and she can't wait in this traffic. "I will call you later. I'll walk from here." She gets out of the car and runs to the top of the street entrance. She takes one look at what is before her and her heart sinks.

"Oh fuck, Ruth."

Chapter Twenty-Five

IF YAH WANT MA BODY

It's been over an hour since Ed and Eva followed the Bentley to the park. Eva is sitting on top of the dry-stone wall watching Ed clean out the sheep's water. A few of the new mothers and their lambs are snuggling in the field around them, minding their own business. Ed, however, hasn't stopped talking about the Bentley, it's driving Eva mad. She looks at her watch, trying to politely hurry him along.

He's gone from the Bentley to every expensive car he can think of. "What about if pimped the tractor up and we can sail about in it, Ev? We could record it and it would be like one of those YouTube shows, put Halifax on the map and that." Ed is really enjoying his little motor world, but she just wants to dunk his head in the trough. "I think you should shut up!" Eva can't listen any more about men and cars.

She loosens one of the stones from the wall and thinks about her Mum while Ed continues to entertain himself. What is her Mum's problem? She wonders. Yes, she wants her to be happy, but can't she just not have a man for one second. Everything is a mess, let the dust settle from Dad, he doesn't seem to be with anyone. Not in that little box of a flat anyway, it reeks of lonely bloke in there. Give it time and then jump back on the horse.

"Why do you think my Mum can't get by without a man?" she asks Ed, throwing stones at him. He pretends for a moment he hasn't heard her. She's not gonna like what he thinks. "Ed," she calls again and throws a bigger stone. It hits him on the shoulder and she shrugs as if to say sorry. "Ev, you just got to let people do their own things. Your mam deserves to be just as happy as you are." Eva looks surprised by his answer. "Wow, I never expected you to be the peacekeeper," she laughs at him. "Yip in years to come they will all be asking old Ed for advice," he chuckles to himself and gives a wink to the sheep.

A Range Rover slowly makes its way along the narrow road. Eva notices the private plate. "Shit, it's Gran," she frowns and gives Ed a stern glance. "Play nice."

"Always a nice guy, me. Maybe she won't notice me if I hide behind the sheep," and he puts his hood up and squats down. "Here comes 'Grim Granny," he whistles and goes back to feeding the sheep. Martha pulls up in front of Eva and winds the window down slowly but keeps the engine running. "Hello beautiful," she smiles at Eva but gives a 'I hate you' look towards Ed. "You on your way home? I see Dad is at yours, nice of him to say." Eva only knows this, as Ed has previously told her earlier. Martha tuts at Eva. "He's out with some of his schoolmates in town but looks like there's some kind of accident near the town centre, taken me an age to get though." She looks at Ed again. He stares back at her, and Eva waits on an altercation to happen.

"Why don't you both come around for some tea or dinner tomorrow?" Martha gestures towards Ed, who looks a little petrified now. Surprised by this invite, Eva says, "We'll see how things are on the farm. If we have time, we'll try." Martha nods and sets off down the lane towards her farm.

"That was unexpected." Eva turns round to Ed, who's watching Martha drive away. He looks back at Eva. "You're being naïve, Ev, always a plan with these types." She frustratingly shakes her hands towards his face. "And am I one of these types?" Eva starts to get defensive. Why has he got it in for Gran? He leans over his shovel, smiling at her, he kind of loves raging Eva. "They broke the mould with you, love," he says, giving her another cheeky wink. She loves it when he's being cocky.

"**D**o you think my Dad will be with the Friday night lot?". She seems a little worried about him as he wasn't himself in London. Normally he's giving her the world, but he seemed to want to get rid of her. "Nah, he'll be with those business types who go to the Irish bar after their shift." Ed puts the feed and shovel back in the van. He doesn't like how they mess Eva about. "Stop thinking about them lot, and concentrate on yourself, it's what they are doing. They are selfish, you need to do you. And me several times a week," he grabs her hand. "Have you enquired about changing your degree yet?" he sits on the wall next to her. She shows him her emails. "Already in the process of doing so, nothing is going to stop me. Not Granny, Mum or even Dad." Ed jumps off the wall and puts a tune on his phone.

"Come on then, it's Friday, let's get the party started," he takes out a few cans from the boot. "They will be warm," Eva screws her face up. Ed points to the chiller in the boot. "Come on Ev," he starts to dance and pulls his top up showing his toned pale body. "If yah want ma body," Ed gestures for Eva to come and dance. She throws her head back and pretends she doesn't want to join him, so he beckons her with his finger. "Let's have a wee roll in the hay. Nobody's about. Granny-pants is way gone," she laughs at him. What at sight. The poor sheep don't need to see this.

His phone rings with a police siren ring tone and the music stops. Ed answers. "Wayno mate, what's up?" Eva can hear the voice on the other line, sounding distressed. Ed's voice gets serious, and he looks at Eva. "What's up?" She's concerned.

"Something has happened near your Mum's shop, an accident, that's why the traffic is mad." Eva jumps off the wall and moves towards him. "What accident? What's happening? Tell me Ed?" He hangs up the call. "I don't know, let's just get in the car and go see. Come on, Eva, grab your stuff," he hurries her into the van.

E va looks up into the sky as a police helicopter can be heard circling around the town centre. She tries calling her Mum first but there's no answer, so she tries her Dad, and he answers but sounds drunk. "Hey Eva, what's up baby girl."

"Dad, what's happening in town, something about an accident near the shop? Dad, can you hear me? Dad is Mum, okay?" Eva looks, and the call has been disconnected as the signal is not very strong in the lower valley. "Fuck, Ed, nobody is answering, and nobody is telling me anything." Eva is blaming herself for shaming her Mum earlier.

"Try your mam again on my phone," he flings his mobile across the car to her. She looks at it, but there are no bars. "No point, still no bloody signal."

They both stare at each other not sure what to do but Ed just keeps driving and taking the back roads hoping they can try and avoid as much traffic as possible. He knows all the sneaky routes and will cross a few fields if he needs to. As expected, Stump Cross is rammed so he heads back up past the Shibden and towards the dry ski slope and down through Boothtown. It's still mega busy, but at least the traffic is moving in that area. "We will park at the top and walk down," he says, pushing through the traffic, honking his horn so people will move. Eva starts biting her nails again, how will she cope if anything has happened to her Mum? This is Dad's fault if he hadn't messed up, she would be with him at home right now safe. Not with the blingy man and not in the town centre.

They park up and run down into the town centre, making their way towards the shop. Eva's still trying her Dad who's not answering at all. Her phone suddenly starts ringing and she slows down to answer. "Stop Ed, it's Mum," she answers trying to speak but she's out of breath.

"Mum, what the hell is going on?" No answer. "Mum, answer me? Mum?" Hannah finally speaks,

"Eva." All Eva can hear is the soft sound of sobbing as an ambulance siren wails. "Eva, it's not good. Are you near?" Hannah says, sounding exhausted. Eva stops and listens to what her Mum has to say. She puts her hand to her mouth in disbelief. "Mum, we are on our way," and she runs again towards the shop.

Chapter Twenty-Six

AMONGST THE DEVASTATION

Noise is all there is. Hannah stands amongst the chaos. Her body is still, fear has frozen her. She closes her eyes and then opens them once more, hoping that everything she sees before her isn't real. It's her mind playing tricks, taunting her once again. But that's too much to ask for. She slowly takes in the devastation which surrounds her. All she has is dread and her legs tremble.

The grey damp cobbles looking back up at her are now awash with running water as it splashes against her trainers, and she watches as it continues to flow between the streets below her. Flashing lights and people in hi-vis suits approach her. They look blurry to her and all the colours blend. She steadies her feet as her gut clenches.

"Miss, you can't be in here. This is a restricted area." He pushes her back and continues to put up cones and a 'do not' enter barrier.

She stumbles back, holding her stomach tight, and feels sick. A white van lies on its sides, hazards flashing and is dipped halfway down a hole with water gushing like a fountain up through its engine. The firemen surround it scratching their heads, but to Hannah's amazement, there are people taking pictures, and yes, selfies next to the van. What the hell is wrong with people? She is now struggling to breathe. A man in the crowd is laughing with his mates and everything seems so bizarre. She wonders if she's dreaming.

Hannah pushes her way through the crowd to the other side of the van and ducks under the barriers. Again, a policeman approaches and tries to refuse her entry. "My bloody shop is in there. I am coming in there whether you like it or not." She is not taking no for an answer. The next thing Hannah hears is a familiar teary Scottish voice say, "Officer, she is with me." Ruth runs up and cuddles Hannah, crying uncontrollably. Hannah checks over Ruth making sure she's unharmed.

"I thought the worst for a moment, my whole world just stopped." Hannah chokes up and squeezes Ruth tightly. Ruth laughs uncontrollably, Hannah thinks she must be in a deep state of shock. "Ruth, calm down, stop laughing, crying, I don't know which." As Hannah looks up, Arron, the delivery bloke they use from time to time comes round the side of the van. He has a wound on his head and blood over his face and is just calmly drinking a cup of tea. He bangs on the van wheel with his bandaged hand and looks at it with some kind of pride.

"She a tough old girl. We've got into many scrapes, but I think she's not going to survive this one." He sups his drink, shaking his head, and now looking at his van like a part of him has died. "But at least she went out magnificently. A moment that will go down in history." He now beams and looks at Ruth and Hannah. "Come on, ladies we are going to be famous. They'll be talking about this for years. I reckon I'm going to get more than £20 out of this, Ruthy," he comes over and hugs both of them.

Hannah is baffled. From behind the van, it looks like a major incident, so how can these two be enjoying this. "For fuck's sakes, the two of you need to look at what's happening. Is either one of you two or anyone else injured?" Arron sniggers like a kid.

"Oh, there is at least a few hundred!" Hannah can't catch her breath again. Ruth wipes the tears away from her face and clutches Hannah's face in her hands looking at her with a serious expression. "You need to see this for yourself." She takes Hannah by the hand, over to the other side of the van. Arron raises his arm and guides Hannah's eye to view the many casualties left to fend for themselves on the little cobbled street in the centre of Halifax.

So many of them scattered and left amongst the devastation. Nobody is yet tending to them. An entire job lot of vibrators are currently rolling down the street as the burst water main washes over them. Hannah, Ruth, and Arron stand at the top of the cobbles and look on at the rubbery rainbow water show before them. A sight Halifax is sure to never forget. Ruth turns to Hannah; her face has never looked so proud. "It's beautiful, isn't it? Out of great devastation comes a wet dream. I feel like I've created a gay pride rubber slip and slide." She grabs Hannah's hand and swings it from side to side like a happy mother proud of her little children.

Hannah pulls away. She is furious. "What the hell have you done, Ruth? He could have been seriously injured or someone else?" she paces back and forth. "It's funny to you but this will bloody close us for good now. You could've just left the street closed." Hannah's feet are now soaked from the water, and they are being moved away from the van and into the café across the way.

Ruth sits with her head down nursing a coffee, Arron hasn't moved from the window taking pictures of the police trying to stop people entering the area and taking selfies with the vibrators that are still scattered all over the place. "Hannah, look, I'm sure that copper just pocketed one," she laughs. "He did, I am telling you, he did." Hannah can't believe what she's dealing with. "Maybe you should go home now, Arron, the police don't need you and nothing can be done until tomorrow." He thinks about it for a minute.

"Nah, this is the biggest moment of my life. What if the telly turns up?" With that, he goes outside and starts a Facebook live feed.

Ruth looks up from her drink and clears her throat. "I didn't think about what could or would happen, I was just pissed off and thought they were out to get us." She looks up at Hannah like a scolded child. "They are after us more now, Ruth, and we now need to be prepared for the shit that follows." Hannah walks up to the window and watches Arron take pictures with people like he's a local celebrity. "Never seen someone look so happy. You've at least made his day," and she pats Ruth on the back. "We are royally fucked now, aren't we?" Ruth takes out her vape, looks at it, then decides not to use it.

Roger, who owns the café, comes over and puts down two cream buns. "These are on the house. I will be honest. I grabbed a vibe, only as a memento. When it dries out, I'll see if my boyfriend likes it." He rubs his hands." Ruth and Hannah turn to each other and burst out laughing. "Glad to be of service," Ruth shouts to him. Ruth then stops and thinks. "I hope we haven't caused Roger problems. Councillor Jeremy has been giving him grief as well." Hannah doesn't understand why he would do that. She looks at Ruth confused. Ruth can't believe Hannah's naivety. The business council has become the witch hunters recently. Roger politely smiles from the counter; Hannah had no idea. But she had enough of this witch hunt.

"The girls at the hairdressers are being given letters as well, so I think there is more to this than what you think, Ruth. Something bigger than that twat's prejudices. I mean, they are not even a proper council, just a local business committee." Hannah remembers seeing Martha with them. What are they up to?

Coming out of the café, the van has now been pulled out of the hole and Arron is inspecting it like a loving parent. The water has now been turned off and most of the vibrators have collected at the bottom of the street. The police and fire service look at the girls, trying hard to stop sniggering. An officer approaches to give them an update on what's happening. "The street will remain closed until a full investigation has taken place. Looks like someone moved the sign." Ruth lowers her head. "We will need statements from you both and the driver," he points over to Arron, who's face lights up like he's been asked for a television interview.

Harsmit is standing next to the van. His face says it all as Hannah catches a glimpse of him. "All good here?" he shouts.

"Oh, yes. Just another normal day at work." Ruth shouts back and Hannah scolds her and tries to talk, but he gets in there first. "I will leave you to it." He makes a 'I will call you gesture' to Hannah, then looks around at the devastation again and leaves. Arron runs up with a carboard box all excited. "Look, I saved a few. These are unharmed." Hannah and Ruth just look at him. He grins and tenderly looks down at the box. "These are my little survivors."

Chapter Twenty-Seven

FRIDAY NIGHT LOT

"**S**hots and five pints of Guinness." Stu hits the bar like he's like tapping on a drum. The bar tender, George, gestures to say they've got the order and starts the Guinness train flowing. Dylan is shaking his head; he's not feeling it tonight. "I want just a half and no shots, Stewart." Stu ignores him and looks to the bar staff.

"No half allowed here. He wants a pint." Stu then bends over and whispers to Dylan. "Staying at your mams, you'll need those shots." They both laugh, and Dylan looks at the shot and downs it.

The bar is packed with Friday night drinkers who've finished their busy week, and ready to let off a little steam. Stu puts his hand into his pockets and produces a wad of £50 and £20 notes. He leaves a £50 on the bar for the drinks, flicks through his notes and pops them back in his coat pocket. "You'll get jumped flashing your cash about mate," the smallest member of the group chirps up. Stu ignores his comment. "He just wants to look like Billy Big Bollocks," says George the bartender and takes the note, holds it to the light, and walks to the till. Muttering 'wanker'.

"Full of sass, that one!" Stu is well chuffed to have his mate back out on a Friday night, but God, is he depressing. "Fucking hell, Dylan, put a smile on it, not often you're out with the lads on Friday these days now you're a southern ponce." Dylan takes a drink of his Guinness and shrugs. He's not in the mood and doesn't care what anyone here thinks. They are childhood mates and Stu now runs a few used car dealerships in the north but does some bits on the side for Burnside Holdings. "Suppose it's a little cheaper up here," says the little bloke. Once again, everyone ignores him. "Not staying out too late, got a lot on my mind." Dylan is now nursing his pint. The little bloke's trying his best to get Dylan's attention. "A lot of noise happening outside, got a road closed and been an accident but thankfully there's no casualties." The little bloke tries to squeeze into the conversation, but they just freeze him out.

The little bloke manages to worm his way between Stu and Dylan, holding his pint tight to his chest. "See your Eva's messing about with that Ed lad," he pipes up. Now for the first time, Dylan turns his attention to him, the little bloke looks nervous. "Is there something you want to say about my daughter?" He towers over him.

"No, no. I was just saying," he cowers. Stu intervenes.

"Piss off over there, you little perve," he hands him £20. He takes Stu's money and disappears to a group of women at the other side of the bar, who notice him and block him out of their group.

"He's a little twat, that one. But that Ed's an all-right lad. Knew his Dad, solid bloke. Salt of the earth type. Ed works hard and causes no trouble." Dylan sniffs and pushes his glass away; he doesn't have a problem with Ed. In fact, he likes his work ethic. His only concern is with Eva. "It's just so much has gone on and I don't want Eva messing her life up because of me." Stu signals for another two drinks. George gives him the finger. Stu grins, taking it as a signal for flirting. "Look, you've got a lot on, but Eva is strong, and I believe, like her mother, that she knows her own mind."

Dylan wishes he was so certain; nothing feels good now. "Yeah, maybe," Dylan pretends to agree. Stu tries to make him feel a little better. "The person to blame is fucking Richard, all matey like he's your 'bro' most of your life and then causes shit, I mean, faking an affair?" Dylan looks around.

"Keep it down, Claire has fucked off and I now can't prove that happened." Stu grabs his arm to show support.

"But mate, you now know in your head," and he points hard into Dylan's forehead, "that you didn't do it, no matter what anyone says. One day Hannah will see that." Stu is trying to get Dylan to talk about Richard, as he also owes Stu a load of cash. "We all got blindsided by him, good at his job, a mate for years, so you all pushed Hannah to the side, and you know mate, she held that against you." Dylan knows that well as she didn't talk to him for weeks.

"Yip, that was my first big mistake." It's getting louder as the music has been turned up and more people are coming into the bar. "So, he didn't go to his own mam's funeral. Did you speak to him?" Stu is taking no prisoners tonight, he, like everyone else, wants some answers. "If I see him, I'd flatten him." Dylan's now getting wound up. "He emailed Mum, that's all I know." He doesn't want to be questioned. "Look mate, I am off for a piss," he makes his way to the toilet, but when Stu isn't looking, he heads to the exit. He needs to get out of there. His head is banging.

He jumps in the first taxi outside. The driver had to take the long route back to the farm because of the commotion in the centre of town from earlier. He's telling Dylan everything that has happened, but Dylan is too busy scrolling through his phone. Then he hears the driver say, "A bloody landslide of dildos, closed Halifax down."

"What did you just say mate?" The taxi driver repeats.

"Dildos. My friend had a street full of Rubber Rabbits, you couldn't write it, I didn't even know there was a sex shop in Fax." He then messes with his sat nav.

Dylan decides to call Hannah, but she doesn't answer. Frustrated, he bangs his head against the window. "Mate, you break, you pay." The driver warns him. "Sorry," Dylan sinks back into his chair. Pulling up at the farm, he pays over the odds for being a dick. He walks through the back garden and staggers a little up the path. *All out to get me,* he thinks. *Everyone. The lot of them.*

He rests on the stone bench overlooking the overgrown pond. "Fuck you, Dad," he says out loud towards the pond. Noticing a spade leading against the fence, he goes over and grabs it. "I will finish what you started then, didn't even get to say goodbye or see your face, I could do with talking to you. See what a mess things are without you." Tears run down his face, and he forces the spade into the ground. He digs and digs, taking his frustration out on the dry earth until he hits something hard. Clearing it with his hands and wiping muddy tears away from his face, it looks like pieces of bones and something small and shiny. He stands up, he's been digging for a while and is now standing knee deep in the dirt.

A light goes on in the house and Martha appears at the back door with a shotgun and trying to tie her dressing gown up. "Dylan, what you doing? I thought it was the bloody foxes after the chickens again." Dylan freezes and doesn't know what to say, he just cries, and Martha puts the gun down, draws him into her stomach and hugs her son. "It's all going to be alright; we are a strong family, and I will get you through this. Mum always cleans up the mess and makes everything alright." She strokes his hair and sits in the mud in the middle of the pond with him.

"Sorry, I dug the pond, I just, I just," Dylan continues to cry.

"Shush my boy. It's all okay." Martha strokes his hair again. She looks at the pond and all the mud now over the pathway and then, she catches something she didn't expect to see. There's something shining in the moonlight.

She stares at it with a sense of remorse, but then her face changes and all that can be seen is purpose in her gaze. "Let's get you to bed before all the horses start stirring. There's one thing I can guarantee, my boy, is that things always look better in the morning." She helps him up, and he leans on her as they walk to the back door. Martha turns back around and takes another look at the pond. As they walk, Dylan leans on her for support as she struggles to take him into the house. As they enter the house, Martha looks back towards the pond one more time and whispers, "Sweet dreams, my love."

Chapter Twenty-Eight

POND LIFE

Why is the building vibrating this time of the morning? Dylan's head is still banging from last night and all he can hear is the reversing sound of some van. It's loud high pitch beeping intensifies his pain. He sits up and opens the bottle of water next to his bed. He feels so dehydrated. He thinks he shouldn't have had that shot. Definitely not as young as he used to be. He felt like a child waking up in his old room. You would think Mum would've re-decorated by now, it's still full of all his old rugby trophies. He should be spooning with Hannah, tickling the back of her neck. Having Saturday morning sex while Eva is away with her mates. That's how it's supposed to be, not laid here in this hell.

He can smell earth and looking at the small armchair, he notices his clothes are covered in mud. His memory is fuzzy, but he recalls the pond and not much more than that. Standing up the pain is more intense. Seeing himself in the mirror, he pats his gut and sighs. *Bang, bang.* The noise outside is getting louder, so he pulls the blinds and stands at the window in his boxer shorts. Looking over the extension, he sees a small digger working its way in the pond area. Max, a local lad and 'his Mum's minion' has his earphones in mindlessly digging away. Dylan pops his comfies on and heads down to see what's happening outside and try to figure out what he was doing in the pond last night and why now is 'Minion Max' digging it up?

"Hello, Father." Eva is sitting at the kitchen table, arms crossed and behaving like she's his mother. Martha is washing up and looking out at Max digging while the radio is playing trying to drown out the noise. Little Alex comes up and gives Dylan one leg lick and goes back to beg for toast at Eva's knee. "I was calling you all night, only one drunk reply. There was an accident at Mum's shop. Do you suddenly not care anymore?"

"I know, I tried to call. Well, I think I did anyway." Drinking is not good for him he hasn't drunk this much since *that* night. "Is she ok?" His heart hurts.

"Yes, but Halifax is not, it's now plagued with dildos." Eva gives Alex a little toast. He rubs his eyes to wake himself up. "Dildos? I don't know if I want to hear any more." Dylan sits down at the table and pours some orange juice. "No, I suppose you don't. Got a headache?" Eva is on his case. She just doesn't get it - you would think he would stop drinking so much considering the amount of trouble it has caused.

Martha hasn't acknowledged the conversation and she's still looking out the window while squeezing the side of the sink trying to control her frustration. She watches the digger moving soil about. "You okay, Mum?" Dylan goes over to look out the window. "I'm sorry about last night." Martha dries her hands on the tea towel.

"All is good, and it's about time I sorted the bloody pond out. Max will be working on it for a few days. Then I have specialist called Reece coming over from Manchester to look at it." She continues drying her hands and Dylan stops her. "It's okay, I know it's reminding you of Dad." She half smiles at him.

He goes to walk back to the table and remembers a little from last night. "What you got buried out there? It's like an animal cemetery," he laughs as he sits back down. Eva gulps slightly on her toast and tries not to think about what Ed said. Martha playfully hits Dylan with the tea towel and looks back out towards the pond. "You know, cats and dogs."

The cobbled road to the shop is still closed, but on this chilly Saturday morning Hannah and Ruth have no choice but to get on with the clean-up, one hundred products had littered the tiny street last night and it had even made it onto local news and gone viral. Arron will be pleased. However, most of the stock has now gone, either washed away or taken by watchers, Friday night drinkers or removed by the local police, who, given the circumstances, remained professional. Ruth notices John, who sometimes sleeps outside the shop, with a black bag, helping to clean up with some of his mates. "You guys up for a brew?" she shouts.

"Always up for a hot one," they reply, laughing and continue to bag things up. Eva appears at the bottom of the street with bacon and sausage teacakes and offers them out to everyone. They all sit on the curb and tuck in. "Just took Alex for a walk to Grans. Dad was there completely hungover and oblivious to all this. Gran was also behaving oddly. And for her, that says a lot," Hannah pulls a face, thinking old Martha's enjoying this total shambles. "Go on, I am sure Martha had plenty to say." Eva thinks.

"No, she was more interested in the pond being dug out, never batted an eyelid when I mentioned it." Eva put more brown sauce on her bacon.

"So, Eva, you, Ed and this course," Hannah starts.

"Please don't have a go Mum, I came to help out." Hannah puts her brew down and sits next to Eva, glad she came to help her old Mum out. "No love, not a go. I just wanted to say. I am proud of you." Eva smiles. "You had the courage to say that your life had been planned for you and stand up and shout for what you want. That, as a daughter and young independent woman, is all I can ask for. So go and be everything you want to be." Eva is trying to hold back tears, but her eyes deceive her. She knows her Mum can finally see her. "I love you Mum, even though you make shit choices," Eva hugs her Mum. Hannah looks around. "Yip, might be shit, but at least they are always fun."

A black Audi parks at the top of the street and the two business councillors look towards the small group. They get out of the car and start shaking their heads. "Look, the vultures are out on Saturday morning to see what they can pick at," Ruth blurts out. He gets his notepad out and starts writing in it while the other takes pictures on their phone. Hannah takes control of the situation. "Ruth, Eva, in the shop now. Everyone thanks for your help, it's appreciated," she shakes their hands, looks up at the vultures and follows the others into the shop. They wait nervously, looking at each other in anticipation of the councillors who are about to come through the door.

"We knew this was coming. It's our fight, Ruth, and we can't let them win now we are aware it's not just us they are being heavy-handed with." Hannah and Ruth look at each other in agreement. Eva continues to eat her bacon sandwich, watching and waiting for a movie show down. Ruth watches the door, her eyes narrowing as the danger approaches.

The door opens, and the vultures walk in. Counsellor Jeremy is smiling like he's won the lottery. It's his finest hour and finally he's got them cornered and exactly where he wants them. "Well, this is a mess. What did you say in our meeting? Your shop doesn't bother anyone? Well, looks to me like it bothers the entire town and nearly caused injury!" He rubs his hands, ready to go in for the kill. Hannah calmly pulls a book out from under the counter. "Do you know what this is, Mr Jeremy? You are undeserving of the title you have given yourself," she looks him dead in the eye. He looks back at the other councillor for some kind of reassurance, but she gives him nothing, you can tell she dislikes him. "Unless it's a pardon from the King, you're done Mrs Burnside, or should I say 'Ms.'"

Eva lets out a loud "oh, you just didn't!" His eyes are beaming.

"It's Hannah, always has been, always will be. Marital or any kind of status means nothing to me." She walks over and shoves the book hard into his chest. He looks down and around the room, still unsure what's going on. Ruth walks forward. "I knew there was something about your name that didn't sit with me, so I did a little digging. It turns out that your address is used for many deliveries from our site," she rubs her finger down some PVC suits on display. "That address orders a wide range of things that would even shock the likes of me!"

The second councillor is sniggering in the background. "So, what is it you would like to say? Or shall I visit your wife with a little fantasy gift basket?" Hannah produced a basket onto the counter. "Would you like it gift wrapped for an extra £9.99?"

He says nothing and again looks round, terrified he has now become the prey. "Don't let the door hit you on the way out." Ruth then pulls the address book from his chest. Hannah steps forward. "Whatever you are up to, regarding terrorising this street, I will find out. After all, we are kind of like local celebrities now, aren't we, Ruth?" The second councillor backs out the door and disappears. Jeremy stands his ground a little longer. "We will see," he says, and leaves.

Chapter Twenty-Nine

SUNDAY SOAK

The Shibden Valley is a place of splendour. You couldn't live in a better area for long scenic walks with many paths to follow. You'll constantly stumble over history with breath-taking views around each turn. The hillsides change from field to forest on a whim and the bees pollinating the wildflowers make it even more enjoyable. Today's walk, however, was a muddy one as it rained heavily the previous night, but Hannah loves a Sunday morning stroll. It was her and Dylan's 'thing'. Regardless of how busy he was, they got up and walked for hours, then returned home to share a bath. Suppose it's just her 'thing' now.

After a quick stop at the Shibden horse box for a cup of coffee on her way back, she realised that the girl on the box knew about Friday's little incident because she sniggered a little the moment Hannah appeared but she didn't say anything. But she couldn't say the same for the fellow walkers and horse riders along the trail, shouting, "You're a vib!" at her, but it was pleasant enough banter given the circumstances.

Alex has rolled in an immense number of sheep poop and Eva isn't around as she loves hosing her down in the drive as Alex chases the water. So, it's up to her. Hannah gives her a good scrub, but Alex is more intent on chasing the birds nesting in the hedgerows. They have a little tug of war as Hannah tries in vain to dry her off, then puts down her bowl of breakfast. But Alex just turns her nose up at it and goes off to lie in the smallest bit of sunshine coming through the window. "Not good enough for madame?" She's just mad because she didn't get a sausage at the horse box.

Now it's her turn to soak. She turns on the hot tap of the roll top bath in her en-suite. A Sunday morning soak is one of her joys. The bath sits in the middle of the white-tiled room. It's plum coloured with a roman mural print on the bottom half. It was the one thing she had custom made for the renovation chosen and designed by herself, a Hannah one of a kind. Her little piece of paradise. A skylight above allows her to lie back, soak, and look at the clouds. Rubbing her stiff shoulder, she puts some muscle soak into the bath and places her hand in the warm water to start the bubbles going. She makes her way back downstairs and heads to the kitchen.

As much as she prefers wine for soaking. Sunday is a 'cuppa in the bath while listening to music day'. Checking her phone while she's there, she sees another gif pic from Harsmit about the incident. Hannah was a little terrified he would pull away, due to the commotion and the press coverage. But instead, he has rather enjoyed the drama. He taunted her all-last night with silly pics as they chatted on the phone. Never did she think she would connect with someone with a sense of humour, a lot like her own. It's always endless laughing with him. He may wear the flashy clothes, but in essence he doesn't take himself too seriously. With Dylan, it was an uncontrollable passion, and from the beginning, he was all about his family business. In hindsight, she wonders if she was just too naive for him. And the betrayal has made her feel her life has been a lie for so many years. Maybe he should've had someone more in line with family ways, as his mother always said.

She was so busy looking at her phone she knocks over some dried flowers on the side table. Petals are once again all over the floor and thinks she best get them picked up before Alex decides to chew on them. Going to the small cupboard at the front door to get the vac,

Hannah notices her tote bag from last week. Normally she empties it, but she must have been too busy or a little tipsy from the wine that day to do so. Taking the vac and the bag out, she set the bag on the kitchen table and vacs up the petals and nips upstairs to turn the hot tap off.

The bathroom is a little steamy, so she opens a side window to let some air in but notices a figure kind of hiding outside the gate. She makes sure she's covered and bangs on the window at them, and the figure moves on quickly. "Bloody perve," she says out loud. That's the problem with big windows, anyone can see in. The house is next to local trails, and it's not the first time someone has been standing, staring in at her in the last few months, but never this close.

Back downstairs, she makes sure all the doors are locked. While the kettle boils, she empties the tote back on the table. The envelope she picked up the other day falls out in front of her. Ripping it open a small key falls onto the wooden surface with a number 37 on it. "How bizarre," she mutters, picking it up to look at it. She pulls out a note that is also inside. It's written on purple paper. It reads:

Dearest Hannah,

You are the brightest girl, and they know that. I wish I had the courage to give you this before now but, I admit, I was weak and have always protected them. A mother must protect her child no matter what the circumstances. Something I think you would understand. This key will show you a little glimpse of what has been hidden for far too long. Be careful greed is a powerful motive.

Your friend, Maggie x

P.s you had always been my favourite prodigy. I am sorry I allowed this to happen.

Hannah holds her hand to her heart, a letter from Maggie, but why? She flips it around to see the post date. Posted two days before she died and delayed due to insufficient postage. Picking up the key again and looking at it, she notices the key ring has a name of a holding facility. What is this all about and what has greed got to do with it? So many questions. Hannah puts the key in her dressing gown pocket and pops the letter in a side drawer.

She looks up at the open plan room window and is startled by the figure standing directly in front on the other side of the glass. She is frozen and Alex then jumps forward, barking at the it. What she believes to be a male, hesitates for a second, then runs away. She grabs her mobile phone and calls the police.

It's no longer worthwhile taking a relaxing bath so she pulls the plug, heads downstairs and unbolts the front door to let the officer in. "I have checked the back and front of the property and had a drive around, but nobody's about. If someone was there, they are long gone now," he says as soon as Hannah opens the door. "Have you looked at the CCTV?" he asks.

"Doesn't seem to work. I have contacted the company to have them investigate it. The Wi-Fi here is never good so constantly having someone out to look at it." Hannah doesn't let him in, as he seems to be a little rude and she can tell he has no interest in being there. "We will keep you updated, but it could've been someone walking who got a little lost or having a nosey at the house. People off on these Lister walks get themselves lost all the time." He seems to be itching to leave.

"I presume you want to be somewhere else, so I will let you get off," she says sarcastically. "Now, ma'am, we take everything seriously and will conduct a proper line of investigation. It's just we are incredibly busy and don't have much manpower at present, but I assure you that I have taken considerable notes." Hannah looks him up and down.

"In that case, goodbye," she shuts the door in his face. He seems a little miffed and talks into his radio while he heads back to the car before giving the building a quick once over in case she's watching him.

She hears him drive off and bolts the door again, feeling a mixture of scared and intrigue. How strange she keeps seeing a dark figure and this letter suddenly appears. Maybe it's the business council trying to scare her. These strange things started the moment they began to put pressure on the business. She goes to the big glass window and looks out at the view. Reaching into her pocket, she pulls out the key and holds it up to the daylight. "What secrets are you hiding, my little friend? Do I really want to know? Yes, in fact yes, I really do."

Chapter Thirty

HEARTBEAT

Ruth recoiled at the strong, smell of the sanitized surfaces and the sound of people rushing about whilst sitting on a tall, high-back uncomfortable plastic chair. She's never been keen on hospitals since being a kid because she spent far too much time in them, to the point they felt like a home from home. Her Dad died early in her life and each day her Mum would pick her up from school and they would spend the afternoon, into the evening, on the ward with him. Her dinners were often served from the vending machine, or her Mum would sneak cheese sandwiches onto the ward when money was tight.

Collin, her Dad, worked for Jock Burnside in the Paisley branch and her Mum, Brenda, was also a secretary there. After her Dad had passed on, Brenda struggled financially and then lost herself to drink. The Burnsides stepped in and encouraged Brenda to let Ruth go to University and work with them to help pay the bills. Brenda treated them like gods, but Ruth was always wary as her Dad always said he did things he wishes he could take back working for a Burnside.

Ruth never saw much of what her Dad talked about working in the office, but she always kept her eyes open and her nose clean. Some of the older blokes could be heard talking about debt collecting in the good old days with their fists. And rumours of back street deals with officials always went around the office. As for Brenda, her not so loving Mother, well, that's something Ruth doesn't talk about.

Waiting on the powder-green chairs, Ruth looks at the leaflets and stares at the others sat in the waiting area alongside her. So many women and of varying age groups, some with supporting partners, making her feel incredibly lonely and others like Ruth sat alone, trying to hide deep into the chairs, hoping nobody notices them.

"Would you like to come through?" A friendly voice address Ruth. She smiles politely but her legs turn to jelly, and it takes her a few seconds to balance herself, to be brave and stand up. A young girl who's barely seventeen shares a look with her. The look that only a woman who has ever been in this situation can understand. Ruth's ice queen heart breaks for her as she follows the nurse to the cubicle.

T he curtains are powder-blue, with small prints of the local area are closed tightly behind them. The nurse wipes the bed down and asks Ruth to lie down and get herself comfortable. Staring at the nurse, all Ruth can think of is how much plastic she has on. An apron, gloves, and mask. So much white plastic for one person. She's used to black PVC.

"Now love, is it just you or have you brought someone with you today?" asks the friendly nurse, who's all smiles and politeness.

"Just little old me, I can look after myself you know, perfectly capable," she starts to get defensive.

"No, love. I just meant did I need to wait for anyone else before we start with the scan?" she looks at Ruth like she's heard and seen all this before. "Sorry." Ruth's a little embarrassed now. Could she be more pathetic. "So, if you can just pull up your top up a little and buttons down slightly, I will pop a little towel over each." The nurse helps so the clothing is pulled back properly. "This will be a little cold but will not hurt in the slightest," she spreads the gel over her stomach. Ruth wishes she had asked Hannah to come with her, but all of this is so messed up to explain.

Messing with the machine and changing her gloves, she turns to Ruth and puts the scanner across her tummy. "Just a little push about until we find the right place, nothing to worry about, you're doing really well, love." But the nurse then pauses and leans look at the screen. She then starts pushing Ruth's tummy a little harder looking closer at the black and white image. Ruth's never felt dread like this before.

"What's wrong? Tell me? Please," she begins to panic.

"Nothing's up lovely. In fact, everything is perfect." The nurse smiles at her reassuringly. Ruth is growing to like this lady now. The nurse then turns the screen around for Ruth to see, "Say hello to your little baby, a strong heartbeat and great measure for twelve weeks."

The world completely stops, and the little fuzzy black-and-white screen shows a little shape of a tiny head. "Mine?" Ruth quietly whimpers. The nurse pats her leg and Ruth who's smiling, tears up. Her heart is full that the little life on the screen is hers and she vows she will never be like Brenda. Everything and anything else mean nothing at this moment. She thinks of Zofia and how over the moon she will be. "Can I get a picture?" she says quickly.

"Of course, it's the best part of this," laughs the nurse. She wipes the gel from Ruth's stomach and Ruth takes the tiny picture from her and clasps it to her chest. "Thank you so much, you do a wonderful job," she says, thanking the nurse again.

She makes her way out of the building, holding the picture to her chest. It's like a dream and she doesn't want to wake from it. What she didn't want turns out to be all she has ever wanted. Something that is hers and all she wants to do right now is kiss Zofia and tell her the news. But the problem was that she is yet to find her, knowing Zofia is in fact still in Poland. With whom and where, she doesn't know. There's been no response from the people she has emailed, but she remembers she hasn't checked since yesterday. Immediately, she gets her phone out to have a look, but she stops in her tracks.

Across the way she sees that bloody councillor outside a building, and he is talking to a man showing him and others around. Perhaps she should go over and give him another piece of her mind. But the man he's with looks sort of familiar to her. He turns his head. "Harsmit," she says in disbelief. She would notice that snappy dress sense anywhere. He notices her and looks like a deer caught in the headlights. The councillor also notices her, and he quickly goes inside as Ruth marches across the street towards Harsmit. Crossing the road, Ruth has no interest in him, she's after the councillor, but Harsmit stops her.

"Not saying hi?" he steps in front of her path.

"Hi, why are you with that piece of shite?" Direct as always is Ruth.

"Yes, I am aware of the issue you have had with him, but this is just a business venture," he leans in as to gain Ruth's confidence. "Would it be okay if you don't mention my being here, as it's a business thing and I don't want to upset my partners?" Ruth is unsure of this, but she also doesn't want him mentioning seeing her near the hospital. She stops and looks at the building and then looks at Harsmit. "I won't tell if you don't," He gives her a thankful smile.

"Agreed." He puts his hand out for her to shake it, but Ruth just stomps off towards her car.

Another time she would have told him where to shove it, but nothing is going to get in the way of her feelings and this moment of joy will not be taken from her by anybody. Getting into her car she once again looks at the scan picture. Clutching her stomach, her eyes feel heavy again, to think this little creature is growing inside of her is a blessing. Rifling through her bag, she pulls out her phone and opens all her email apps. There's nothing, so she decides to check the spam mail. Scrolling down just in case she sees a Polish heading on one of the emails. She quickly clicks on it, full of hope. The email is from one of Zofia and Ruth's friends. She has seen Zofia recently and can perhaps help Ruth track her down. This is a good sign on this day of all days.

She looks down at her stomach and says, "You wanted to be with both Mummies, didn't you? Rest assured, I plan to find her, and I will not let both of you down this time." Ruth pulls her seatbelt over her. "Now let's tuck you in and keep you safe."

Chapter Thirty-One

INVESTING FOR HALIFAX

Councillor Jeremy of the VBC (Voluntary Business Council) is continuing his tour of the derelict factory space. Backed with VBC investment, but needs developers and outside money to make the project happen. Advertised as 'Investing For Halifax'. He keeps repeating the words 'local housing for local people' and there are plans up inside the building showing pictures of what it will look like and how many flats should occupy the space along with a communal area and shared parking spaces. It is a public tour but mainly to attract local investors as the bidding will go out to tender the end of the month. Jeremy is tripping over himself, trying to impress the investors he has invited.

Harsmit returns from his run in with Ruth. His business partner is waiting for him to join the tour. Councillor Jeremy had noticed him talking to Ruth outside when he tried to avoid her advances. He grabs a drink and approaches Harsmit to find out what has gone on. "You seem to know the lady well outside?" Harsmit stays professional as always.

"We are here today to look at the facility and decide, like the others, if we wish to invest our time and money into such a venture. Whom I talk to is my business." The councillor waves his arms apologetically, terrified to lose such a high-profile investor. "I meant no harm, only making conversation." He fixes his tie nervously. This is a big day for him. He has worked hard in securing these high-value business types with plenty of cash to invest. "A lot of interest has been shown in these local projects to help the community thrive, with vast competition wanting to make their mark on Halifax," he gestures to the group from Burnside Holding PHL who are looking over the planning structure and talking amongst themselves. "They have a finger in everything and are keen to see Halifax progress to the next level. But we are keen on new blood joining and taking us further." His ambition sees no end.

Harsmit's business partner walks forward. A well-dressed female in a white tailored suit with long dark hair. Her Prada heels slowly chiming on the concrete floor. She doesn't look vastly impressed. "You keep mentioning helping the community but as far as I can see your retail price for these apartments is high! So, you are effectively pricing them out of the market, keen as we are to promote local growth." She shows a look of distaste as the councillor again adjusts his tie. She continues, "It all depends on whom you are helping, it seems to me this is project to benefit the rich and keep the low-income earner out."

Walking over and picking up a leaflet, she looks at it and then fixes her gaze on Councillor Jeremy. "It is not in any means the project you have advertised. In fact, it's very misleading." She hands him the brochure. He hesitates and gulps to wet his throat. "I assure you our market price is correct. People need to work harder and earn more. Big changes are coming to these local streets." Harsmit puts his hand out and shakes the councillor's hand with a firm grip. "Thank you for showing us around." He looks at his partner and she smiles politely, not even trying to hide her distaste. "We will be in contact if we feel this meets our criteria." The lady in the white suit puts her bag under her arm and nods to the Burnside group as she knows them well.

Dawn Blackburn from Burnside Holdings nods back and makes her way over to the councillor as Harsmit and his business partner leave. "Inviting outside sources in now, are you? Martha Burnside will be so eager to hear this! Considering your plans to wipe out her ex-daughter-in-law's current business premises and build parking." He doesn't answer and scurries off to greet a new prospective investor as they make their way through the door. "Bloody Burnside spies," he whispers to himself as he goes. Dawn goes back to the group and they all glance at Harsmit as he leaves the top floor. He politely gives them a wave as the lift doors close. He knows when he is being watched.

"You're playing with fire." Lucy, Harsmit's's business partner finally addresses the situation with him in the lift. "You will get burned. Those are the kind of people you don't mess with. There is no community here, just greed." Harsmit laughs at her accusation, knowing she does like the game. "That's why I brought you, always sniff these things out." The lift stops and they walk out, and Lucy looks up the street. "And the woman you had the intense conversation with earlier, is that the new squeeze?" Harsmit screws his face up.

"No, no. Firstly she's not for me and secondly, I am not her type." She clasps her bag with both hands and goes forwards towards him "So you and me can pick up where we left off?" He backs off and put his hands out.

"That, as you know, was just grown-up fun, nothing more." Lucy flips her hair back. She's not offended, she likes to play games. "Mainly cos I am too good for you."

They walk back to their cars parked near the building. "You know, I could have given you a lift over," Lucy says to him. "But I am guessing you have other business. I hear you've been spending time with a little blonde over this way, care to share?" Harsmit clicks for the car to open and winks at her. He has been keeping his relationship private for the time being. "A man has to be allowed some secrets." Lucy sighs, she's not one to back down and is determined to find out. "Multiple dates I heard, so this one must be kinda special to warrant this kind of attention. Not seen you this attentive since...," she goes silent and realises she may have overstepped the mark. Harsmit is a long-time friend, and she wouldn't hurt his feelings for the world. "It's okay," he says, now looking at her with a soft expression.

Lucy leans against her car door and plays with the window. "She was lovely, your wife, and your kids are lucky to have a Dad like you. I just hope this one is worth it." Harsmit walks over and gives Lucy a massive hug. "You are a good friend, as well as a demon of a business partner. But it's too soon for the kids to know. I am just taking it easy with Hannah for now, she doesn't want anything too much either." Lucy abruptly pushes herself up off the car and puts her head to the side. "Hannah?" she looks around, registering where they are. "We are in Halifax, please don't!" She looks furious with him; how could he be so stupid? "No, you didn't? Harsmit!" She pushes him back with her hands and hits him aggressively with her bag. "It's fucking Hannah Burnside, isn't it?" Lucy paces about the car park, frustrated with him.

H arsmit sits on the bonnet of her car and shrugs his shoulders at her. He knew this was going to happen but won't be told what to do by anyone not after the last few years he's had. Lucy pushes him again. "All you can do is shrug. Hannah Fucking Burnside! She's married into the Burnsides. You idiot!"

"It's cool, they are getting divorced," he shrugs again, completely oblivious to why Lucy is so upset, considering Hannah is a free woman. "Are you thick in the head. The Burnsides don't play nice and once 'The Gunner' hears you, a business advocate, is fucking his wife, ex or not. It's not going to end well." She just can't understand his lack of concern. Surely, he is aware of the Burnside's hard business reputation. "You're talking like this is some kind of mafia cult, and who calls themselves Gunner? Is that a joke?" He gets up and straightens his jacket. "Lucy, you're over thinking-babe!" Lucy points her finger straight into his face. He needs to listen to her. "Don't fucking call me babe!"

"Sorry, sorry," Harsmit pleads with her.

"You've done it this time. You need to stay away from her as of now!" Lucy demands.

How dare she presume to tell him what he can and can't do. Harsmit slams the car door hard. "For your own good and the company, they will not let this go. No wonder they stared at us this whole time today. They probably already know and will attempt to bury our business. It's not just about you!" She is livid with him, solely thinking about himself.

"I think you have said too much Lucy and don't go running to the other partners telling tales. My personal life is that personal." Harsmit is enraged that she should tell him how to behave but Lucy is not leaving it there. "If your personal life affects our business, then the partners need to know. I will not say, but you need to. I can't let this ruin all of us. You have until tomorrow to speak to the to them and at least address the issue." She walks to her car, gets in and slams the door then she speeds off out into the traffic.

Harmit looks at his phone. Hannah is calling. He stares at her picture consumed with anger which burns into his mind. He dares not answer and cuts it off, gets in the car and starts hitting his phone on the steering wheel. He turns the engine on for a moment and then off again. Gripping the leather steering wheel, he screams.

Chapter Thirty-Two

BURNSIDE HOLDINGS PHL

Martha has just walked through the office door and her assistant is eagerly waiting on her. "Pads and pens are on all the tables, I have set teas, coffees and soft drinks up on the stand for you, Mrs Burnside." Megan, the office junior, has spent all morning making sure the boardroom is ready for today's Tuesday meeting. Old Jock Burnside never liked a Monday meeting. Tuesday was his day, which allowed the staff a Monday to get back into work and clear their heads. This seemed a more productive use of staff time for him. The tradition has since stuck and not one Monday morning meeting has been called in the history of Burnside Holdings PHL.

Martha rolls her eyes at the boardroom and says, "The carpets are looking dated," she drags her stick along them, pointing out the worn areas to Megan, who notes down every word and agrees with everything she says. "Most places no longer have carpet, Mrs Burnside. Much cleaner to have some kind of flooring down, I could arrange a few quotes?" Megan is always willing to please the head of the business. Martha, who's enjoying the attention and agreeable behaviour of her staff, knocks on the radiators with her stick. "Perhaps a complete modernisation of the office. Call on our designers and have them work something up for the board to look at." She then ushers Megan out of the room, while telling her to stay near as she will be needed.

The board members arrive and begins to help themselves to teas and coffees. Each one making an attempt to interact with Martha to gain favour. "Is Dylan not joining us today? I hear he has been up for a long weekend?" Bob Littlewood stirs his sugar and confidently sits on the chair close to the head of the table. He is always trying to impress. "All board members are called today. This is a fully closed meeting, Bob. He will be here in good time, however I am sure I don't have to explain myself to you!" Martha bangs her stick against his chairs as she seats herself at the head of the boardroom table. Bob fixes his notepad in front of him like a child who has just been told off.

"You're in my seat, Marathon Runner," a voice announces from the corridor. Bob picks his coffee up and moves to the end of the table. Dylan is fully suited in navy and is clean shaven for today's meeting, the first he's attended in person since the move to London. He sits down on the chair next to his mother and gives Bob a stern look. He notices the two empty chairs where Richard and Hannah once sat. He brushes down his shirt and sips on his glass of cold water. Martha glances at him and notes his nervous demeanour and his look towards the empty chairs.

Megan closes the door and sits outside watching for any signals from Martha. The board is silent, waiting for Martha to start the meeting. She bangs her stick against the table leg twice. "I will not keep you all long this morning. I am aware it has been a strange few months for our company," she now looks at the two empty chairs. She needs to remind Megan to remove them. "Things always change and we, as a company, have to change with them and advance forwards but always be on top of the game." Her gaze rests on Bob, who looks startled. "On top and I repeat again, on top," she bangs her stick. "Perhaps I have been too soft, or a little side tracked since Richard's absence and the death of his mother, my dear friend Maggie." Dylan gives her no eye contact and instead plays with his glass. "We have more competition these days and as far as I can see you are all rolling over and letting them in. Dawn reports that a Bradford-based initiative is undercutting us and with budgets being squeezed for most companies, we are letting this company take our jobs."

Dylan finally speaks. "What Braford company? You keep saying this. Looking at the figures we are sitting fine," he points to his notes, baffled by what she's saying. Martha doesn't like him questioning her. "Sitting fine is not the way this company works. Your father never sat fine in his life, and we will be on top!" Martha's face turns a little beetroot colour. She notices Megan outside the door, who signals with an envelope.

Bob then tries to stand up and say a few words, but one look from Martha and he changes his mind. "This is not the way the company should be anymore. The world has changed, and we need to change with it." Dylan decides to challenge Martha. He's sick of this old-fashioned behaviour towards business from her. Martha pushes her chair back aggressively and walks towards the window and gestures for Megan to come in. Megan arrives, still holding the envelope, and hands it to Martha then leaves again. "You have been so consumed by your broken marriage and I didn't want to have to do this, but your wife and ex board member is consorting with the enemy, Dylan." With that, she throws the envelope in front of him. Everyone at the table looks at each other and feels uncomfortable but intrigued. They love the family drama.

Dylan looks at everyone waiting in anticipation for him to open the envelope. He tears at it, pulls out some photographs, and sees Hannah with Harsmit. His heart sinks. He can't look at his wife with another man, and now he can understand how she felt at this moment when she saw pictures of him and Claire. "Why are you showing me these?" he demands. Martha sniffs and replies,

"Because he is part of the Bradford group. Mr Patel, who's your wife's current squeeze, is hustling in on our territory." Dylan looks down again at the pictures. He doesn't see him at first, only Hannah. Her face is glowing, and she looks happy a look he misses, and then he looks at the next picture and his blood boils. The man is kissing his wife. He slams the pictures on the table.

"Everyone out accept Martha and me, now!" He commands. Nobody makes any attempt to disagree, and the board members scurry out of the room faster than little mice. He watches them all run out and turns his attention to Martha. "How dare you do that in front of the board members, you have no right to mess with my marriage." He points hard at the photos.

"Your marriage is over, but what you clearly don't see is your soon-to-be-ex has been targeted as part of a plan to mess with our business." Martha is determined to make him see things her way. Dylan laughs at her. His mother has lost the plot. "What the hell would she know and why, just why?" he covers his face with his hands. "Why would she do this?" and he throws the photos onto the floor. Martha moves closer to him and squeezes his shoulder. She now thinks she has her son's confidence. "She wants revenge. She will never believe your innocence and a hurt woman needs some kind of revenge." He thinks long and hard. He struggles to see Hannah being this person. Megan comes back in and waves her hand for Martha to leave the room.

Sat alone in the boardroom, the clock ticks seem louder and Dylan feels alone and powerless. He bends over and picks the picture of Hannah up off the floor. "What have I done to you? I love you and will protect you no matter what." His words are soft, but then he looks at the picture of the male again and his rage grows stronger. Anger sweeps across his body, his head banging with noise, visions of them together, moments of tenderness that should be his, nobody else's, and he can't control his actions now as jealousy consumes him. Grabbing his car keys, he marches out of the office.

"Dylan, stop! We will do this together," Martha shouts after him, but now he can only see his own rage and his path is now clear. Kicking the fire exit door wide open, he leaves the building as Martha hobbles behind him. What has she unleashed?

Chapter Thirty-Three

THE RED DOOR

E d is standing in the shop scratching his head. He's not a hundred percent sure what he has got himself into. Eva has managed to persuade him into helping her mam and Ruth move stock from the shop to the storage unit. But Eva's mam has not turned up yet, leaving him upstairs amongst a pile of products he'd rather not be touching. Not because he's prudish at all, he's game for almost anything, it's just more than he bargained for today.

It's safer for him to be up here in the loft space, as Ruth is in an overfriendly mood one minute and then the next barking orders. He's terrified of her normally, but today he's petrified. Eva appears with a clipboard. She appears to be enjoying the power it's given her. "Ruth has written down instructions on what needs doing. She says you're not listening to her, Ed." He puts his hood up and tries to drown out his frustration. "Looks like we are boxing most of the stuff up and taking it to the warehouse, as the shop will be closing." Ed scratches his head again, this place is doing his head in. "Confused Eve, I thought they won the war with the Business Council and the local press love the whole 'dildo waterfall' story."

Eva can see he's beginning to get irate. She loves it when he's a frustrated Ed. It's cute. "Not closing, just refurbing, so I am told," she says, enjoying his agony. They pack up the boxes, which Ruth has already marked up and ticked off the check sheet on the clipboard. Ed notices the door in the corner of the loft. It's small, red, and very narrow, a bit like a cupboard door. "What's in there?" He loves little treasures in old buildings and his eyes widen at the thought of what's behind the door. Ruth appears, and when she sees him by the red door, she shivers. "We don't use it, creeps me out. We found strange old dolls and shit in it when we moved in." She shakes her body, trying to get rid of her chills. "Go on let us have a look?" he pleads. Ruth rolls her eyes. She's not going in there for anything. Some things should be left alone. Ed isn't interested in her warnings because he's too curious. He's seen loads of abandoned places videos. He gets his phone out and begins to record and talks into the camera quietly, as if he's a ghost hunter. As he slowly opens the small door, it creaks, and he goes down on his hands and knees to crawl inside.

It's dark and he can feel the spider webs softly brushing against his face, but there's a small window that opens onto the roof of the next door's building. It's wedged open with a brick. He shines his torch from his phone over the little room. Looking around, he jumps and drops his phone, quickly picking it back up, he shines it to where he thought he saw movement. With panic in his voice, he shout's, "Ev, Ruth, you need to come see this, someone's been sleeping in here!" He helps Eva and Ruth through the door and shines the torch again towards the window. "What the fuck?" Ruth puts her hands to her mouth in utter shock. Ed goes over and shines his torch on the floor now. "Look, there's a fresh sleeping bag and empty snacks, made a right proper home. Is it that homeless guy?". He kicks amongst the bag for glues. Ruth thinks for a moment and she's sure she saw them outside this morning with their tatty sleeping bags. The one on the floor looks brand new.

She closes the window tight shut, whoever it is won't be getting back in. "Ed, can you get something to block this, and I will report it to the police?" Ed nods while still recording the scene, but his phone dies and he is peeved. Ruth notices Ed has kicked over an funeral order of service from Maggie's funeral and she quickly hides it from Eva and Ed. "Let's get out of here, it still gives me the creeps." She ushers them back through the tiny red door.

Outside, the road is still closed, so they put the boxes on a trolley and take them down to the van at the bottom of the street. They brush the cobwebs from their jumpers. "Don't you think Ruth is being weird?" Ed asks Eva. "Weird? She's all kinds of weird. That's just her." Eva is used to her family and can't see anything different; Ruth is the same as she has ever been to her. "Nah, me guts telling me something is odd, just not sure what, and it's not just the red door." Ed rubs his belly. All this help and nobody has offered him any grub yet. "Maybe you're just hungry?" Eva pulls on his t-shirt and pats his belly. It makes a hollow sound. "Maybe I am hungry for some of that ass," he slaps her on the bum and they fall into the van passionately kissing. Ed stops and strokes her face. Her family are crazier than his. "I am telling you Ev, something is amiss in that shop and she's hiding things." Eva pulls him closer, he's like an old granny at times. "You're so hot when you're in detective mode." He smiles.

"Oh, I can get down with a little bit of role play."

B*ang!* The side of the van shakes and they both look up. Ed jumps out of the van, thinking Ruth has followed them. But Dylan's standing outside the van and his face is fixed on Eva. Ed steps back, he knows when not to mess with someone and presumes he wants a word with him. But Dylan's attention is solely on Eva. "Your Mum in there?" he asks, straight to the point. He looks up towards the shop. Eva struggles to get up and out of the van. She's not fourteen and sneaking out anymore, so why can he not just back off and leave her be? "Just Ruth and someone sleeping in the loft room, apparently." She says sarcastically, as doesn't want his drama. Dylan tries, but fails, to control his temper and not scare Eva. He looks at Ed, and guesses "Another one of her blokes perhaps?" Ed steps back again and then put his arm around Eva. He's seen that temper before and has no intention of letting Eva and himself get harmed. "Nope, not me Gunner, I am all hers. Promise." Eva shakes him off.

"What the hell Dad, back to being the local bully, are you?" Dylan's annoyed she's challenged him but sees her mother in her. "So, she's not here?" his tone softens with her, and Eva sharply replies,

"No." He glances at them both, looks up at the shop as Ruth comes out and walks back off to his car.

Ruth runs down the cobbles, noticing Dylan walking away. "What the hell is going on? I can hear you from up the street." Ed's eager to tell and excitedly blurts out, "Gunners on the warpath looking for Hannah." Ruth looks again, but he has gone.

"Is it entertaining for you?" Eva scolds Ed. He huffs and goes round to get in the driver's seat. "Do you know what's happening?" Eva puts her hands on her hips and questions Ruth. Perhaps Ed is right. Ruth seems shaken and a little guarded. Ruth shakes her head. "I know your Mum thought someone was at the house on Sunday morning and now the loft room." She shows Eva the funeral service sheet she found. "I found this upstairs. Don't tell Ed, sorry Eva, but he's a total gossip." Eva looks at Ed, this she knows, but again he's so cute. She walks over to the passenger seat and gets in. "All, okay?" he asks sheepishly.

"Is it ever?" she replies. "Just drive!"

Ruth hurriedly gets her phone out and rings Hannah. She answers as she's on her way up the street, sounding a little out of breath. "Okay, Dylan's just been round and doesn't look in a good mood. What's gone off?" Hannah stops on the street and thinks. She hasn't seen him since the funeral or taken his calls. Ruth sees her from the bottom of the street, hangs up the phone and goes back to the shop. She looks upstairs at the red door to the loft. Her thoughts are confused. Why Maggie's funeral service? And who would want to sleep in there?

She hears the door chime and heads back downstairs to see Hannah and show her the loft room. But it's not Hannah at the bottom of the stairs, it's Dylan. And Ruth knows that look, she's seen it before, and it reminds her of his Dad, Jock 'the Gunner' Burnside. She left her phone upstairs so there's no time to warn Hannah. She just hopes it's not all going to kick off.

Chapter Thirty-Four

THE STAND OFF

If Halifax were a location in a western movie, the saloon would be based here at 'Pleasure Not Sin'. Ruth is watching Dylan's every move, while Dylan, fingers itching for a verbal fight stands in the middle of the floor, his suit slightly creased and his hair messy. It's a standoff and neither are willing to back down. His face looks bitter, and neither of the two say a single word. It's like they have played this scene before. Ruth is finally the first to move as she slowly makes her way to the bottom of the steps. He follows her moves and circles round to make sure he has a clear view of the shop and blocks the doorway.

"Where is she?" he hisses. Ruth Rolls her tongue in her mouth and tries answer. But the door opens, and Hannah enters the room. She looks at him and then at Ruth, whose eyes are telling Hannah everything she needs to know. Closing the door behind her, her heart slightly in her throat, she can sense the tension in the room and that this visit isn't a friendly one. She's seen this temper before, she can see it in his face and since Jock's death it had mellowed, but was always simmering under the surface. She knew all this when she married him, and she accepted it because the parts she loved won her heart. But this version of him is the one she feared the most. The one that nobody could reason with. Not even her. "You've been seeing Harsmit Patel?" His fist begins to tighten and he's trying all he can to hold back his anger. Hannah looks at Ruth for reassurance. "Whom I see is now up to me," Hannah answers firmly. Ruth finally opens her mouth.

"I am asking you to leave Dylan, you're angry and I don't care why, but we don't want this here. I am asking for old times' sake to please go!" her eyes are pleading in the hope he sees a little sense and leaves. He sees nothing but red. "One thing I never thought you were was stupid, Hannah, but you've been had and in turn, that reflects badly on me." Dylan looks at Ruth but is addressing Hannah. How can he seriously be this stupid? His arrogance is pathetic to her. "Wow, you think I care what reflects bad on you? You didn't seem to care when what you did broke me and everything around us." Hannah's consumed with hurt as the grief of his uncaring attitude hits her hard.

Ruth once again steps closer. "If you and Hannah need to talk, it should be with solicitors. You're not hurting her anymore." Ruth steps in front of Hannah as this has gone too far. The Burnsides have taken too much. "Hurting her? She's been messing with a business adversary. Fuck knows what you have been telling him." Dylan finally moves towards Hannah; Ruth blocks him, and he stumbles and pushes her. "Don't you touch me again or I will scream." Ruth's now scared and thinking of her baby. She backs off. Never did she expect him to lay a hand on her. Dylan steps back, ashamed of himself. "I would never hurt you like that." He leans around to touch Hannah; she jumps back terrified of him. "I fuckin love you, don't you see? It's because of me he's been allowed to worm his way in and get close to you. You've been played, Han." He's desperate for her to listen to him. Hannah can't believe what he's saying, but she not going to let him see that. "You don't know what love is, you're just protecting the money and company name, you sound just like your Mum."

With that, Martha enters the room as she'd been following Dylan to find out what she had unleashed. Hannah turns to her. "Oh, look who it is. Proud, are you? This has your name written all over it. You know exactly how to push his buttons." She turns to Dylan. "And you just let her. Our entire relationship has been manipulated by her and your family's business. It never stood a chance!" Hannah cries. This is all too much. These people are monsters.

Her crying is not sorrow, it's anger and frustration. No matter how much she feels free for a second, they pull her back. Ruth walks to the front door. "I think it's time you all leave. If I have to, I will call the police," Hannah looks at Dylan. "Take a look at what you have become, a puppet for your mother. Everything you wanted to get away from." Martha shows no emotion, no defeat. It's not in her nature and for the first time speaks. "You best to remember, girl, that everything you hold dear is from Burnside money. All you have is this," she points her fingers around the shop. "As we wouldn't touch it with a bargepole. But Dylan was adamant to let you have something that was your own. Even his father agreed, despite my doubts." She opens the door. "Think yourself lucky we still let you live in that massive house you have turned into a brothel, as that too, is a Burnside property."

Hannah's overwhelmed. The tears for her marriage run down her pale skin. She looks at Dylan longingly, but with disappointment. How could it all come to this? That man that was once her everything, and now he's just her enemy. Ruth gestures to Dylan to get out. He looks at Martha who is already on her way out of the shop. "It's still stands Hannah; you have been played. Watch your back with him." He moves past her and gently rubs his hand against hers. She pulls away from him for the first time ever in disgust. Her heart is not just broken, he has annihilated it from existence.

She runs towards Ruth for a hug, but Ruth puts her hand out to stop her. She is shaken but needs to speak. "There is something I need to tell you, Han," she looks guilty but knows she can't keep this from her. "I believe they speak the truth about Harsmit." She hangs her head not wanting to hurt her friend more, but it must be said. Hannah's shocked she would even dare to agree with the Burnsides. Ruth is always slagging them off. "How could you say that? You hate them" She points outside, as Martha and Dylan can be seen talking.

"I saw Harsmit with a creepy councillor looking round some properties. He asked me not to say," she blurts out all in one breath.

Hannah can't believe what she is she's hearing. They all just want her to be miserable. "You just don't like him and want to keep me to yourself, Ruth. You prefer it when I am miserable." Ruth scoffed at the accusation. "Fuck you, Hannah!" she shouts loud enough to wake the dead. "It's always about Hannah. Shows you barely take a second to see what happening to anyone except you. Poor blonde, cute Hannah with all these blokes after her." Both are as angry as each other, tensions are running high. They have never fought like this.

"Say how you really feel, why don't you? You're just jealous I had something that you never had." Hannah stops, she shouldn't have said that. She didn't mean it. Her mouth ran away with her. Ruth stands wounded by her words and wipes the tears from her eyes with her hands. Never has she felt so let down by her friend. Years of friendship and she has never been this brutal with her. "Well, you're on your own now. You need someone to pick up the pieces of your broke life? Find someone else." With that, Ruth grabs her things and runs out of the shop. "Stop, Ruth, please, I didn't mean it." Hannah shouts at the doorway into the street after her, but Ruth doesn't turn back. She keeps going and Hannah shouts again, "Please, I love you, don't leave." Ruth hears her but shakes her head and continues down the street, out of sight.

The shop is now quiet, just Hannah stood alone looking at her reflection in the full-length mirror. 'Well, you've don't it now haven't you,' she addresses her reflection. 'Scared them all away. Some things never change. They love you and leave you all in the same breath.'

Chapter Thirty-Five

I'VE GOT THE KEY

Pulling the shutters down on the shop, Hannah is in bits. The two closest people she has ever had a connection with have left her. Her lover, her friend, her family. This shop was a sign of independence - a place of love. It was the route of all that is Ruth. It is now empty, lifeless without her. She wonders if it will ever open again. The metal makes a loud clanking noise is as it hits the ground, and she bends over and pops on the lock. It fights back with her to seal it, a last defiant sign.

The road is now open, and everything around it seems back to normal. It doesn't seem as if anything had ever happened. She moves back onto the street and looks at the building. Her and Ruth's little creation. What they built together was their wee empire, their sanctuary. Ruth was the only person she can truly count on. A person who would lay down her life to protect her, and all she could do was speak to her like dirt. Martha's words kept ringing in her ears. 'Dylan was instant!' 'We let you.' How on Earth did she let them, at every point, have a say in it.

She feels had. Beginning to believe she's always been naive, controlled and manipulated by every Burnside. To think she's allowed them to move her like she was some kind of chess piece. Having always thought she was an independent soul and believed herself to be self-aware. Yet all this time they had been there, and it had been them pulling her strings. She would rather starve and have nothing than let them win or have control over her.

Hannah decides whilst standing on the cobbled street in front of the shop that she needs to protect herself. They can't have it all. She can start over. She has had nothing before and with great perseverance she can do it all again. She puts the shop keys in her pocket, and they clang against something in the bottom of the bag. She rummages in the bag and pulls out the key from the envelope. A car beeps its horn, startling her, and she jumps on to the pavement. She forgets she's been standing in the middle of the road gazing at the building in her own little trance. Looking at the key in her trembling hands, she rubs the engraving on the key ring with her thumb and searches for the number of the brass keyring on her phone. Her search brings up a bank in Leeds. Noticing the closing time, she still has a few hours to get over there before it closes. This key must mean something, or Maggie would not have sent it to her.

One more look at her precious building, she notices the fire escape ladders next door. Funny how it's never really crossed her mind before. You can get onto their roof from next door, that's how whoever has been sneaking in must've got into the loft space. She catches a hooded figure walk towards the ladder who seems to be checking out if anyone is looking. Hannah shouts, "Oi, you what are doing?" The man runs down the side street, Hannah gives chase, but the snicket is clear as she gets there, and he must have jumped the wall into the street below.

'Okay, Miss, to Leeds it is,' she thinks as she gets into her car. Rolling the windows down to try and get some air and wash away everything that has gone down today, Hannah speeds towards Leeds, not caring about the multiple speed cameras.

Her phone rings and Harsmit's name comes up on the screen. Trying not to look at it, she feels angry and betrayed. She presses her foot down harder on the accelerator building speed. Nearly missing a car as she swerves lanes, her heart pounds in her chest she slows down and the call ends. Winding the windows up and taking the junction to join the outer ring road, the phone rings again and this time it's Dylan. "Absolutely fuckin not!" She presses to stop the call, but it rings again, and she cuts it off, now turning the sound down.

Pulling onto a nearby street, there are only one hour parking bays left at this time of day, and she pulls into the nearest ones available. The bank is situated on the next block, and she slams her car door shut and marches towards it with determination. It's a grade two listed building. The entrance has a high gated door, and the reception has a security guard on it. Hannah moves forward to the desk. She gets her phone out as she took a picture of the note left with the key. "Hi, I have a deposit box key and I would like to open it." The girl at the desk takes her headphones off and looks at Hannah like she's about to slap her. "Appointments have to be made in advance for all deposits boxes!" Hannah looks at her watch, this one's a total job's worth. "You're still open, surely you can just let me in, I'm the only one here!"

The girl asserts herself. She's tired of pushy rich people today. "Look Miss, those are the rules, and we have security protocol to follow to protect your deposits, I can look now and make you an appointment." Hannah's frustrated. She can't be blocked now by another pushy know it all. She begins to cry. The girl and the security guard look at each other thinking they don't get paid enough for this. "Please," Hannah pleads through salty tears. The security guard gets up from his post and walks over, he shuts the front door and locks it. "Look, Miss, we can give you five minutes and that's it." The girls shakes her head at him.

"I am having nothing to do with this. You're soft, you are!" She puts her headphones back in. "I just need you to enter the code on this keypad, you then need to walk through the scanner, and I can let you in." He points to an iPad on the wall and Hannah walks over to it. She pushes her hair behind her ear and puts in the code from the note and closes her eyes, waiting for it to say 'it's wrong' but the words on the screen say 'Access Granted'. Amazed and relieved, she puts her bag down to be searched and walks through the security scanner. The guard looks at her bag. He notes the vag pen sticking out and smirks to himself. He hands it back to her. She's sweating buckets waiting to be caught out like a criminal in a movie. The guard walks her down a long corridor filled with cameras and into a room full of tiny silver boxes on the wall. One of the boxes is lit up in green. "This is yours he says, you have five minutes then I'll come back in to escort you out." He leaves her alone in the room.

Going towards the green lit up box, she puts the key in it, and it turns without making a noise. She opens the little door and peeps inside. The inside is not very big, not much can be seen, but several papers. Hannah pulls them out and takes them to the table in the middle of the room and gets out her phone in case she needs to take pictures quickly. It's like the movies, she thinks, as nothing like this has ever happened to her. There seems to be several documents, some deeds, bonds, and official bank papers along with a set of notes that appear to be in Richard's handwriting, which Hannah knows well as he was once an apprentice at the company from being a boy. Martha always seemed keen to not let Richard work with Jock or Dylan. For the duration of his employment, he was kept in the Accounts department with the girls.

Turning the camera on and laying the documents out in front of her, she notices Martha's signature and on the second page document was her name in print, Hannah Burnside, along with a signature. But it's not her signature and she can't remember signing anything with Martha present. Quickly, she looks at the signature on all the documents and it's her name on everyone single one. But these are fake.

Why? She needs to understand them more. She only really has time to read one and is shocked to see what she saw under her name.

She hears footsteps approaching. "Fuck it, you're coming with me," she mutters and stuffs the documents into her bag and locks the box back up. My name, my property, she thinks. What the hell is going on? What has Dylan got her involved with? She knew Richard was a snake. The security guard appears. "Times up, I am afraid," he gestures for her to leave. Hannah walks with him. Once she leaves here, there is no going back from this. She's taken the information from the box now.

The girl on reception points to the iPad. "You just need to pop the code back in on exit. Part of security." Hannah's still confused about what she just read. She wipes her hands on her top as they're sweating and inputs the code. Addressing the girl, she says, "how far is the national bank from here?" The girls rolls her eyes as if it's too much effort. "Oh, I think it's a ten mins walk." Hannah smiles at her.

"Thank you. You have been more helpful than you'll ever know."

Chapter Thirty-Six

OLD FRIEND

The headstone for Maggie's grave has now been erected and in the churchyard, Martha is inspecting the engravings. She brushes some dirt off the top and notices a dead bunch of daffodils laid against it. Picking them up, she then throws them on the grave next to Maggie's. It might be the season, but she can do better than spring blooms. The mud still looks freshly dug and a few weeds are beginning to sprout through. She inhales the earthly aroma and then lays down a large solid box on the ground. It's securely shut tight. She removes the trolley wheels from it and places fresh roses on top of the box along with a small garden pond sign from her pond that has now been dug. Stepping back to look at the full stone, she notices Reverend Brown with another man.

"Morning, Mrs Burnside. A pleasant day and lovely to see you. Looks like the weather is soon to break." Martha nods at him and looks down at the box. "This is the box I want buried in the same grave as my Maggie. It shouldn't be a hard task, given the dirt is still fresh." The Reverend nudges his friend to pick up the box. He doesn't really want to because his back is killing. "Big dog or cat, that is!" he says. The Reverend looks embarrassed and urges the lad to move away quickly. "Sorry, he only helps now and again. Nobody will give him work, so me and Leanne try to help." Martha looks down at the box, then to the lad, who is still unsure about the big box. "Maggie loved this one, apparently." She smirks slightly in a way that makes the Reverend feel uneasy. "Would be wrong not to let them rest together," she nudges the box. "Take it. I've looked at it long enough." The lad bends over and struggles. He walks off trying not to drop it. When he thinks nobody is looking, he then drags it along the ground and then notices the trolley next to Martha.

"I'm sure this must be a hard time for you." The Reverend holds Martha's hands. "Whenever you need someone to talk to, the church is always here for everyone." Martha pulls her hand away.

"I'm not a church person but thank you for your concerns. I want to know as soon as it's buried, but if you don't mind, I would appreciate being left alone."

"Yes, yes, of course, and thank you for your kind donation," he says, tripping over his words. He lowers his head and follows the lad down to the church.

Martha bends down at the graveside and rests her hand on the cold stone. She sprinkles some of the dirt from the pond around the stone. "Well, my dears, it seems you are both finally reunited in death. It's funny that you couldn't be together in life, but you're now closer than ever in death" She pats the stone and stands up. "From all this I am at a loss for a friend now. It seems silly, but who is going to listen to an old fool like me. Trying to keep this family together has been a hard task. Dylan's determined to strike out on his own, young Eva's with a farmer. And Hannah, well I'll still attempt to even that one out. Proving to be tricky, but I always win, and you should know that best of all." She shakes her head. "Look at me confiding in a grave," she chuckles slightly to herself.

Looking over at the church, she sees the lad get the mini digger out in preparation to dig. "If I am honest, I always admired you, maybe even jealous truth be told. I will miss you." This place reminds her of her school days, sneaking cigarettes and a swig of Dad's whisky with the boys at the graveyard, not far from this spot. Just adventures and friends to take on the world together. "But you surprised me, and I didn't see it coming," she hears noise from behind and turns round. Nothing about apart from the digger coming down the path. "Well, sleep tight together, sure it's not the first time." Martha then walks back to her car.

Pressing her keys to open the car, Martha hobbles with her stick along the grey cobblestones towards the car door, when a hand slams down in front of her on the door stopping her entering. A man in a black hoody stands in front of her, looking a little worn with a stubbly beard. The man is Richard. "Thought you had seen the last of me?" Martha turns to him and shows no fear. "You smell awful, your late Mother wouldn't approve." He leans forward.

"You have no right mentioning her name." Martha wasn't fazed.

"Oh, I have every right, considering I paid for the funeral, which you didn't attend." Richard walks away from the car and then walks back and slams it again. He's desperate. "You owe me. The account you said had my money in is dry, you lied." Martha still didn't budge and says adamantly, "Not my fault you blew all the stolen money and had to come back. You must've messed up your accounting then as that was your job. And what do you mean dry? I looked at the accounts just yesterday, all you had to do was wait until today for them to be transferred and closed."

Richard's now panicking. "I waited like you said until the coast was clear, watching and waiting in that shitty loft, but logged on and nothing. All empty and closed so I can't see anything." Martha now panics. She's about to get in the car, but he stops her again. "Nah, I know you have cash and plenty of it hidden. So tomorrow night I want what I am owed in cash. You can meet me, or I will find you." He doesn't wait for an answer, he gets jittery and legs it.

Martha tries to get quickly into the car and drives off towards her farm. Her heart is racing. She expected Richard to be gone and out of the country by now and is worried that that the removal men had found something at Maggie's. She calls Max. "Max, are all the boxes from Maggie's house accounted for?" He goes quiet. "Max, this is important," she shouts at him.

"Okay, no need to shout. Let me look." Max, as always, does what he's told. He looks at the log. "All present and accounted for Mrs Burnside." Martha sighs with relief.

"Anyone tried to have a look?" Max is annoyed she would think he would allow that. "Not on my watch."

Martha looks at the time. "Stay there. I'm coming over."

S he pulls over and dials Dylan's number, but there's no answer. She continues to ring until he eventually picks up. "Do you not get the message? I don't want to speak to you, Mum." Martha pauses for a moment and thinks she has the best intentions for him, but right now, she really needs to speak to him. "It's important. It's about Richard." Dylan angrily responds, "Heard enough about bloody Richard. The only thing I care about is Hannah and I am off to see her and explain about Claire. I know she still cares, and I am not leaving until she listens to me."

"Son, please think it through, leave her to it. What I need to talk to you about is more important." She pleads for him to listen, but he's had enough of her constant meddling. "Not interested," and the phone goes quiet.

Feeling defeated and at her wits end, Martha thinks for a minute. She needs Richard to go, and the only way is to pay him. Dialling another number, the voice that answers is Richard's. "You're not meant to call. We will meet as I said." She won't allow him to be in control, just let him think he is. He's typical of all the males in her life. "Wait, I need extra time and you will have what you want." The line goes quiet and then Richard speaks, "I am done with being messed about with, I want what is rightfully mine, what I was born to have." Martha doesn't want to hear his ramblings or what he thinks his he's entitled to anymore. "Tomorrow night 8 p.m. at the old telephone box near the farm, be near the side wall. You will have all you asked for and more. I promise." Martha waits for his repose.

"Good, because if not, the whole of Halifax will know exactly what's hidden in the Burnside closet." Martha disconnects the call; she has no choice but to comply as Richard knows far too much.

Chapter Thirty-Seven
IT'S ALL OR NOTHING

It dawns on Hannah that life can easily slip through your fingers. In a blink of an eye, her dependable idealistic family life, something she craved, can be just that - an idea, now obsolete. The only consistent thing has been her friendship. If she can save anything, it will be that. "Please answer the phone, Ruth!" She leaves another voice message. It's been a busy twelve hours for Hannah as she's gone over every document from the box. A night of tiresome planning and a morning of putting the wheels in motion. You must accept change. You may not always like it, but perhaps now the universe has bigger plans for you.

Trying to contact Ruth has been so far unsuccessful. She hasn't answered any calls and doesn't seem to be home. Leaving a final voice mail, Hannah can now see Eva and Ed arrive with Alex. "It's all going to be all right. A few details have come to light and yes, I have been played. But not as you think, it's worse than that. I've now taken control of the narrative and sorted us out, because we are the team that will always win." She watches as Eva plays with the dog, she looks happy and that's what matters most, it makes Hannah glow inside. "I love you, little Scottish pain in the arse. You, me, and Eva, our little family. Oh, and the dog." Ending the call, she leans against the full-length glass window. Looks down at her phone again, missed calls from both Dylan and Harsmit.

"Mother!" Eva's voice echoes around the room as she bursts through the door full of energy. Alex pounces on Hannah and she gives her a little scratch on the bum. "I hope those feet are clean," Hannah points to Ed's boots. He realises and removes them. Eva makes her way to the kitchen and pops the kettle on, singing to herself. "Anything from Ruth?", Eva asks while getting mugs out for her and Ed. She tiptoes as just can't quite reach. "No," Hannah quietly replies. She watches as Ed and Eva do their happy little dance together, no cares in the world. Jealous? Yes. But only at their blissful ignorance. "Your Dad is popping over tonight as we need to sort a few things out." Eva stops and turns to her Mum.

"Are you sure that's a good idea? Do you want me to stay and keep the peace?" Hannah giggles reassuringly.

"Not necessary. We need to be alone and talk like adults." Ed opens the side patio door and lets Alex run out into the garden area. Eva follows them with a packet of biscuits and the brews. "You two staying for lunch? I'm nipping back into town, and I can grab some sandwiches?" Ed's ears prick up at the thought of food.

"Right, Mrs Burnside. Sorry I mean Hannah. Pork pie, beef and onion for me." Eva glares at him. He's constantly eating. She bites on his biscuit and sits at the patio table. "Yes, Mum, that would be nice." Hannah then closes the patio door. "Just got a call to make, then I will head off." She closes the door and heads up stairs.

She's put this moment off all morning. It's a call she doesn't want to make, but knows at this moment in her life that it needs to be done. Hannah sits down at her dresser chair and positions her phone, needing the space to talk freely. She then presses the FaceTime button, a conversation that needs to be done face to face, but it's the best she can do at present. It rings for what feels like forever and then Harsmit's face appears on the screen. He smiles softly but he's not full of banter and cheeky smirks like normal, perhaps he has an idea of what's about to be discussed. "Hi" he says, and Hannah sheepishly replies,

"Hi." He looks incredibly uncomfortable, and those movie star eyes seem dull. Hannah knows she must be clear and direct; she owes him that. "Did you know who I was when your Dad asked me to your opening?" Her facial expression is serious, but her voice is weary, and her eyes can't hide the sadness. He looks like he'd been waiting for that question. "Honestly, Hannah, no I didn't, it was only after I became aware, but it means nothing. I am not that kind of person." He leans forward into the camera and his golden eyes, the ones Hannah gets lost in, look so sincere.

So many things have been said to her the last few days, she feels she can't trust anyone. Not even those all-consuming eyes. "I don't know what's a lie and what is truth anymore." She holds back the tears that are threatening to fall. She must remain strong. Harsmit doesn't quite know how to answer that. He wants to comfort her but she's right, it seems to have got very messy and it's not what he wanted. The easiest thing for him to do is walk away, but he doesn't want to. "Hannah, only you can decide what you want and what you believe. I can only tell you that I think I'm in love with you. I know it's only words, but it's my truth." Honesty is all she hears in his words. They look at each other, two people just wanting to be loved, respected and accepted. It's all quiet for a moment. Eva can be heard from outside. Hannah's trying with all the strength she can muster to compose herself and think logically.

"The thing is, I seem to jump from one thing to the next without even stopping to look around at what is happening here and now. I have strong feelings for you, but I need time to look at me and so for now I chose me, if you can understand that?" she breaths out. Harsmit looks heartbroken and runs his hand over his forehead, frustrated by her honesty. "Life is never smooth Hannah, I of all people know that. Please don't listen to whatever is being said, as it's all lies. Ask me anything and I will only speak the truth to you." He desperately tries one last attempt to win her over but for once Hannah is set on her path. "Please just give me some time, there is one thing I need to do and people I need to speak to, but for now, I just need to have no distractions." He nods as if this is all he's going to get for now, but he's willing to accept it. If he pushes, he could lose all chance of ever being with her.

He clears his throat. "If you need me Halifax Hannah, I will be there in an instant, until then be safe and keep a clear head." She tries to speak but her throat is dry and can only manage a reassuring nod, but then whispers, "Bye for now". She moves forward and turns the screen off. Hitting the phone face down onto the dresser, she grabs a pillow and screams hard into it several times. Her face becomes bright red, and tears break free and run down onto the cotton pillow. "Why does it have to be so difficult?" she shouts out loud and flings the pillow back onto the bed.

Splashing her face with cold water in the en-suite she looks at herself in the mirror. "Be strong, be strong. You can do this," she says to herself. Patting her face dry she stays upstairs until the red and puffiness in her eyes starts to calm down, not wanting Eva to sense anything. Applying some make-up to reduce the swelling of her eyes and fixing herself in the mirror, she thinks to herself how funny it is that you can put on the 'all is ok' face even when things turn shit. Maybe that's just female strength or conditioning.

Alex trots into the room and starts digging about the bed and sniffing the pillow. The dog gives Hannah a look as if to say, 'I am here for you'. "Mum, what's going on up there?" Eva shouts. "Ed's getting hangry and that's not a pretty sight for anyone." Hannah gives Alex a hug. She whispers to her 'you get it, don't you' and kisses her furry head. "Okay, just grabbing my bag and I will be off." Hannah also grabs her driver's licence, passport, and proof of address, plus birth certificate. Where she planned to visit today, she's not taking any chances. She's now on a tight schedule, if everything is to go to plan. She looks out the window at Eva who's sat playing with Ed's hair as he plays games on his phone in the sunshine. What she's about to do is not something to be proud of, but she must protect Eva and herself at all costs, even if it means becoming someone she has always tried not to be.

Chapter Thirty-Eight

PASS THE PARCEL

It's 6.30 p.m. and already it's been one of the longest days of her life. Hannah rests herself against the back of the front door and takes a deep breath. She slips off her shoes, kicks them to the side and closes her eyes. Everything is set in motion, she didn't like it, but it is now done. No going back, only forwards. Looking at her watch she realises Dylan will be here in a few minutes. Looking down at her swollen feet she notices there is a letter on the floor with her name on it and bends down to pick it up. As she begins to open it, she walks towards the front windows. Reading the contents, she wearily sniggers and abruptly laughs aloud. Will it never end? She puts it back in the envelope and sits it on the work surface, trying to hold herself together except this letter has not only given her more motivation but increased her will power.

Pouring herself a glass of malbec, she watches at the window. Dylan appears in the distance. She can see his torch moving about like a firefly. He's walked from the farm and as he gets closer, she can see his hair looks a little messy from the wind. He pulls up the collar of his puffer coat and hides his chin. He notices her watching and continues up the gravel path. Hannah walks to the door and opens it before he has time to knock. She doesn't greet him, just walks back to window. Dylan closes the door behind and waits at the entrance hall, warming his face with his hands. 'No going back, Hannah.' She turns around, glass in hand and observes his now timid fragile existence. No longer the overpowering bear that had stood tall in her shop. Her face set and focused on what she must do. "Come in. I suppose it's about time we talked properly, like adults. Not stood in a shop shouting at one another." She seems welcoming, even agreeable. He nods. Perhaps she's seen sense and be willing to compromise on their marriage.

He can't be without her and must find a way to get her back. "I can't let go of you, Hannah. Claire lied, I was set up, nothing happened. You need to believe me. All I want, all I've always wanted, is you and Eva." Hannah wasn't expecting him to be like this after yesterday. If he had said these things eight months ago instead of disappearing. Perhaps she would have been soft enough to fall for it. "What version of Dylan is this today?". She holds out her hand for answers and then puts it back down. She can't help now but to analyse him. "The first one runs away, the second is angry and controlling and now this pitiful one is begging for his family back." She swigs her wine, completely sure of herself.

He notices the wine. "I presume you're no longer pregnant?" He points to the wine. She shouts, "I never was pregnant!" He's deluded, always trying to look for a scenario that she needs rescuing in. Dylan's eyes mist up. "I love you; I need you. I ran away because I could see the hurt in your eyes as you looked at me. I got angry as I couldn't deal with that lying man touching you and now this," he puts his hands to his heart. "Fuck, this now is me being honest."

"Ah, honesty, something your Mum and Dad never taught you as neither of them are honest, are they?" Dylan knows she's right, but he doesn't quite understand what is happening. He will drop everything for her, everything. "Just tell me what you want from me?" Hannah looks out the window as a car comes up the driveway. "You see, Dylan, I have been blind and misleading myself. I love you, and it kills to try not to love you. But because of that I have sacrificed myself, what I want, what I believed, and I refuse to do it any longer." She walks towards him with a mixture of sorrow, regret, and longing. "So, from you, I want nothing, absolutely nothing." She then walks over to the counter and sits at the breakfast bar.

ylan looks lost. This is not his Hannah. He hears the front door go and turns expecting Eva, but Martha is standing there. "Welcome to the party Martha, thank you for accepting the invite," Hannah sarcastically says. Martha walks forward and looks at Dylan and they both share a look of confusion with each other. "Anyone for drink? Nobody?" Hannah draws a look of distaste at both.

"Have you been drinking too much, Hannah?" Martha asks. Hannah throws an envelope on the breakfast bar in front of them. "How about a little party gift for you both?" Dylan picks it up. He has never seen her be so forceful. "No Dylan, ladies first. I am sure Mummy wants to have a look for you." Dylan is getting annoyed.

"What is this, Hannah? Stop with the games." Hannah jumps off the seat and laughs ridiculously. "Yes, a game, it's all been a big game, and the game was always me," she points to herself.

Martha, having seen enough of this spectacle, rips open the envelope and pulls out the contents. She looks aggravated as she scans the contents. Hannah puts down the glass. "Go on then, show your baby boy what you've been up to." Martha grips the papers tightly. Hannah can't control her joy at Martha's discomfort. "We could have discussed this privately." Hannah does a snide smirk.

"Or I could have called the police, but I didn't." Dylan snatches the paper from his Mum's hands. He flips through them, and he genuinely seems to have never seen them before. "What the hell is this, Mum?" He shakes the paperwork in her face. Hannah is quiet and watches as Dylan argues with his Mum. It's giving Hannah a great sense of satisfaction.

"You can both stop; it's all fixed now. After all, it's all in my name, so I have closed the accounts and transferred all your greedy cash into my private account, but I guess you already knew it was missing ex-Mummy dearest?" Martha is stunned, she didn't think the little madam had it in her. The nerve of her. She needs it all back, every penny. What's she going to do about Richard?

"You see, I spoke to a little solicitor myself and it's legally mine now!" Hannah feels very smug and swings on the chair. "You and your minion Richard cooked up a good plan. Use me as the fall guy, fake my signature, so if you want to take legal action, I have made copies." Martha thinks and can't understand how Hannah got this information. She made damn sure she was out of the company and had access to nothing. Hannah watches and can see Martha's mind pondering, trying to work out how she managed to outsmart her. She could keep her guessing, but it's too much fun. "How did I do it? Well, I didn't. Your old friend Maggie sent me the key to her box. She must have found out through Richard, oh and maybe out of spite considering the secret she was forced to hide for all these years."

Martha turns towards the door. "I am not listening to this." Hannah follows her quickly up the hallway, she's got her now and she's not letting go. "So, you don't want Dylan to know Richard was his older brother then?" Martha freezes on the spot; she looks at Dylan. He just stares at her in disbelief. He looks at Hannah for reassurance, but she gives him nothing. "Is this true, Mum? Richard is my brother?" Martha doesn't respond to his question. Her eyes dart to Hannah who's smugly smiling at her. "Mum, Dad was with Maggie?" Hannah moves over to Dylan and mocks him. "Don't be so naïve, Dylan, you've been played! Richard is two years older than you; Jock hadn't even made it down here by then, think of the timeline." Martha is still stood still.

"Son, let's go." He stands in front of his mother.

"I don't understand?" Hannah hands him a birth certificate with Richard's name on it, he reads it aloud. "Mother Martha Crossland and father unknown." He looks at her, his life now a lie. "All these years! How could you not say?" Finally, her dirty secret was aired.

"Dylan, it is complicated. Things were different back then, Son," she whispers. He looks at Hannah and then back to Martha. "Did Dad know?" Martha walks over to the door.

"I am not talking about this in front of that scheming little bitch," and she lifts her stick and points it at Hannah. "Well, since this house is officially mine, you're not welcome here anyway, so be gone, witch," and Hannah walks back to the glass of wine. Martha, not one to let anyone get the better of her proudly walks to the door. "It's not over by a long shot, girl!"

Dylan stands frozen with shock, he looks at Hannah, who suddenly seems like a different woman before him. "What have I done to you?" he then heads out the door after his mother while Hannah downs the last drop of her wine feeling liberated.

Chapter Thirty-Nine

CLEANING HOUSE

Martha walks as quickly as she can back to her Ranger Rover. How dare that little interfering, money grabbing bitch believe she will get one over on her. And Maggie? May she rot in hell. She no doubt planned this act of betrayal before the final curtain, wanting the last laugh. Everything she had done for her. Given her a life many would have killed for. She may have taken on Richard so Martha could thrive, as after all, she had the brains to go far, and Maggie just wanted a baby to love. But Martha made sure she had a comfortable life; it's not Martha's fault Maggie couldn't have kids. Richard was her first and last mistake. A reminder of how a woman's bad decision can haunt her for the rest of her life.

"Wait, don't you dare leave!" Dylan follows her, calling to her to stop. She has taken every step to avoid this moment, so many tactical manoeuvres to allow Richard to be close enough to use him and control his movements. "Does he know? Does he know he's my brother?" Dylan wants answers even though all he had to do tonight was to convince Hannah to love him. But his mother and her secrets, always secrets with her. An entire dynasty built on deceit. "I deserve to know the truth. I have played the good son asking no questions and following in Dad's footsteps. You owe me the truth!"

Martha has heard enough of his whining. Why do these men whine at her? Do they have no backbone? "I owe nobody nothing. We live our lives to survive Dylan and that's what I did, I survived." She shouts but regains her composure. "He's only my son by birth. Maggie looked after him and as far as I am concerned, he is hers." Dylan can't believe what's coming out of her mouth. "You are heartless and cold, you're no sort of mother." He's shouting so much he spits in her face; she shakes it off. "You want *that* as your brother? He set you up. Broke your marriage," she bites back at him.

"Only to get at you, not me. Claire said the pictures had been sent to you! So, tell me how Hannah managed to get them from there?" Martha has now been caught out for the third time this evening, it may as well all come out now. "I wasn't going to be held captive by anyone." He looks at her in disbelief. His own mother prepared to abolish his happiness for money. "So, you throw your other son to the wolves?" She knew he could take it; Burnside's don't fold. "You are a survivor, like me, you don't need her, she can't be trusted." Martha looks back towards the house.

"She can't be trusted? She only did what she needed to do before you crushed her. You're a monster, Mum." To Martha, those words stung. He's spoiled and wouldn't know evil like she has seen. It was also the last words Jock uttered to her before he died. The look on Dylan's face is chilling, he despises her, and it hurts like hell. "Leave Hannah be, let her have what she has taken and that is the one thing I ask for from you. You've taken enough from everyone and don't go dribbling your poison in Eva's ear either." Martha gets into her car.

"You need to see sense, Dylan. That woman has blinded you for too long." Dylan puts his hands in his pockets and stands up to her.

"Do this! Or you will never have contact with me or Eva again and I mean it, Mum, as for Richard wherever he is. I want to meet with him and settle this face to face." Martha lies as if it was second nature.

"I have no idea where he's gone. One email and that's all the contact. I guarantee you will not be seeing him again." Dylan kicks a stone at her car. "I will check into a hotel. I can't be near you." He walks off down the hillside a broken man.

Turning the heaters on full to burn the chill of the evening, Martha's phone rings. "I am here. Don't keep me waiting. Mum!" Richard's tone makes Martha shudder. His voice and everything about him put the devil's hatred into her body. Part of her wishes it were different, but he is a thorn in her side. She curses the day he found out Maggie was not his biological mother. Maggie, being soft, couldn't conceal the truth from her darling boy. They're so much easier to control when they're little, but as they grow, they know too much and become unpredictable.

A fog appears on the road, and it suddenly consumes the barn. Martha can't see much ahead of her. She turns on her fog lights and starts the engine, looking to the passenger side staring at the bag of cash she's prepared for Richard, hoping that this will be their final meeting. After tonight she could get away with not showing up, but he knows more, and she won't allow him and Dylan to meet ever again. So, her path is now set. She knows what must be done to preserve her boy, and all she has built.

The glint of red through the fog tells her she's at the telephone box. She takes a left and heads off the road and out of sight. Parking up she can't see any other cars and she can't tell in the fog who is about. A hand suddenly lands with a thump against the window, and she jumps, opens the door and slides off her seat to see Richard towering over her. The moon peeps through the fog highlighting the whites of his eyes fixed on Martha. "Made you jump a little didn't I, Mum?" Richard looks a little smug. "You, don't like it when I call you Mum, do you, Martha? Well, that's what you are." He always looks self-congratulatory, and she wants to wipe it from his face. So full of his own self-worth and thinks he can manipulate anyone. In many ways, just like Martha.

Holding her ground, Martha doesn't retaliate. "Dylan knows about you being his brother," she finally admits.

"Big brother!" he corrects her. "I bet he's mad at you, isn't he? So many secrets, Martha Burnside. A priest would love you," he looks around. "Did he not want to come and say hi? We could have had a bonding session. Bit of family time." He laughs at himself, but quickly gets back to the business at hand. "I want what is rightfully mine, so where is the cash?" Martha is wary as he seems jumpy and can't stay still, moving from side to side, hands twitching. "It's in the boot and that's your lot, nothing more from this day on." Richard leans in towards her, but she shows no fear.

"Well, I might go and find the brother, crack open a few beers and we can both bitch about what a shit Mum you have been. Who knows, it could be the start of a beautiful relationship." His eyes pierce into Martha's. In true Martha style she says nothing as he rants because he's not the first man to threaten her and probably not the last.

Richard gestures towards the boot. "Come on then, let's see it and I will be off." They walk around, and he's eager to be gone but doesn't trust this woman. She has no understanding of motherly affection. He has seen her first hand with Dylan all these years treating him like a performing monkey. Martha presses the boot to release, and it slowly lifts, breaking the fog. There are small lights in the boot. Richard looks but can't see anything. "Where is it? I can't see any bags." Martha moves behind him. "You'll need to lean in. It must have gone towards the back of the boot."

Richard puts both hands inside the boot and leans on the boot mat. He steadies himself and leans forwards to see if the bags are in the back. Nothing, she is playing games, stalling. He turns around and she has moved closer, blocking his side view. Martha moves close as if to help but she produces a syringe from her pocket, and without hesitation drives it straight into Richard's neck. He goes down quick, no struggle and his head hit the interior of the boot hard. She scrambles and struggles to lift and push his legs into the boot with the rest of his body. He's a dead weight and although her mind is strong, her body is not. She gazes at him as his body lays scrunched up on the plastic boot liner. "Now you should be quiet. No, Richard, you won't be having beer with anyone ever again." She presses the button, and the Range Rover boot slowly closes as she watches to make sure it's firmly shut. Giving it a firm nudge for good measure. Martha pats her pocket, which now has the used syringe in it and walks slowly around to the driver's side. The bigger they are, the harder they fall; some mistakes are not easily fixed but, on this occasion, she is cleaning house.

Chapter Forty

THE END OR JUST THE BEGINNING

Hannah goes back to the bottle of wine. It's dark red consistency is as unclear as the fog outside. She shakily and hastily pours herself another glass and tries to control her beating heart. She feels it's about to break through her rib cage and run off out into the valley, aching to be free. Staring at the half drank bottle, it suddenly offends her, its presence, and its manipulation of her mind just like the Burnsides. She hits it to the side, and it smashes to the ground. What has she become? Who even is Hannah anymore?

She can see Eva walking up the drive from the front door window and quickly grabs a brush pan, sweeping the glass up, throwing mounds of kitchen roll across the spillage. She watches as it absorbs all the wine up and it looks so cold. Stained red - a bloodstain to mark the war that has just begun. She looks for so long that she doesn't hear Eva come through the door. "Mum, I am sure Gran just nearly hit me on the road. She came thundering out from behind the old telephone box people used to pee in like an F1 driver. Should she still be driving at her age? The woman is lethal."

Hannah doesn't look up. It's like the absorption is hypnotising her, drawing her closer, calling her name. "She left here a while back, probably on her way home. She didn't like my company tonight." Eva looks on as Hannah just stares at the floor. "You okay, Mum?" She's concerned as her Mum doesn't seem like herself anymore. She looks fragile, lost, and frozen. Hannah takes a long time to respond, but simply nods and picks up the wineglass and the letter from the worktop. She sits down on the soft yellow chair, tapping the letter, her eyes watching Eva's reflection approach her in the window. "Dad gone?". She sits on the footstool in front of her Mum and puts her hand gently on her knee. Hannah whispers, "Yes," while biting her nails. Eva gives her Mum's knee a soft and reassuring squeeze and moves her hands away from her mouth to stop her biting and get her full attention. "You going to be okay?" she says. Hannah lays her hand on Eva's, rubbing her soft fingers. "We are going to be okay, you and me," she sniffs, raises her glass and smiles, "New beginning for us girls." Eva pulls the stool closer. She has never seen her Mum like this. "Mum, I am worried about you."

Hannah suddenly snaps back to reality. She sits up pulling her open shirt over her shoulders, shivering. "Sometimes, Eva, you got to do things, you know that aren't right, but it's for the good of your family, protecting yourself. I never really understood it till now." She strokes Eva's cheek, her little girl talking to her woman to woman. "You and Ruth are my family. We need each other and I have protected that, for us." Eva's not sure what's she saying,

"Mum, I don't understand, you're making no sense at all."

Hannah produces the letter from her side and reads it again. Eva notices her Mum's expression changes and she seems very sure of herself. The confusing sorrow in her eyes has now gone and Hannah now seems empowered. "What's that you've got there?" Eva nods to letter in Hannah's hand. "It's from Ruth. It was on the floor when I got back earlier." Eva laughs.

"Ruth, she's so dramatic, I didn't know she could write."

"Yeah, she is the queen of soaps," and Hannah laughs, thinking of Ruth's obsession with Dynasty. "But she also needed me, and I was too concerned with my own problems to even notice or give her time to tell me. What kind of friend does that make me?" Hannah put the letter down the side of the chair.

Eva grabs her knees and gives them a good old shake. "Whatever has been said and done, you two are thick as thieves. You're always there for each other, no matter what." Hannah doesn't agree. Eva continues. "So, a few choice words were said in the heat of the moment. Speak to each other, or at least try." She stands up and grabs the letter. "What's she got to say anyway? Can I read it?" Hannah nods and Eva walks back and forth in front of her, reading the letter aloud.

Hi Han,

So, we said things to each other, and they hurt, more than I can say in this letter. I have this habit of letting you take over my life and forgetting about myself at times. Zofia said it many times at first, I thought it was jealousy and now I see it was my reality.

Let me state the truth: you love Dylan, and he loves you. It has always been that way, but that journey has ended, and you now need to find out who *Hannah is*. What does she really want? Because time changes us, and we can't stand still and remain the same.

I need to find what I want and that is Zofia. I was too tied up in our little world to allow myself to commit and I have never met someone like her who sees me for me and knows when I am pretending or putting that tough mask on.

She broke down my heavily guarded wall and do you know what? I am going to let her in. In fact, I am going to spray paint her name all over it.

So, I have gone to find her. No matter what it takes, I shall prove myself to her. So please, because I love you, find Hannah again.

Love the other half of your creative soul.

Ruth x

Ps I am twelve weeks pregnant, and Richard is the sperm donor, yes, it is fucked up. But I couldn't be happier.

"Wow, that's like an episode of Jeremy Kyle!" Eva closes the letter and hands it back to Hannah. She throws herself back on the sofa. "Ruth pregnant? I didn't think that was possible because she said her ovaries had shrivelled like prunes." She shakes her head in disbelief. "And icky Richard, oh you don't think she had sex with him? I feel sick." Eva starts making wretching noises. Hannah stands up. "Don't be ridiculous, they would use some clinic, hopefully." Hannah paces up and down, should she tell Eva about Richard? She must, best to come from her than the lies Martha will tell. "Okay, there is something else." Eva looks up. So much drama in one night there's no need for the telly. "It has to be something big to top that," and she points to the letter.

Hannah put her hands to her mouth like she's praying. "Richard, well Richard, kinda happens to be your Dad's big brother." Hannah sits down fast, waiting for a reaction. "No, never!" Eva's mouth drops, she always thought something was kind of weird with him, always trying to get her grandad's attention. "Grandad that dirty..." Hannah interrupts.

"Actually, your Gran, she let Maggie bring him up, before your Grandad came on the scene." Eva's astonished. She wishes she had recorded this. Ed's never going to believe her. "Shut up, icky Richard is my uncle?" Hannah nods again, she feels like Eva is enjoying this a little too much. "Which means Ruth's baby is, well, your cousin." Eva gets up. "I need to tell Ed this," and she gets out her phone. Hannah rushes to her and grabs the phone. "No, you can't." Eva sits back down, unable to comprehend it. "Does Dad know?" She's finally starting to realise she didn't think about how he must feel.

"He just found out." Hannah feels queasy.

"God, never mind Jeremy Kyle, this is full-blown American tv shit." It's the only way Eva can deal with these revelations at this moment. Hannah laughs at her daughter's amusement of the situation. "Don't make me laugh, it's serious." She gets up and finds her phone. "I need to protect Ruth." When Martha finds out about the baby, God knows what she will do, and Hannah doesn't trust Richard for one minute. He wouldn't have done this if it didn't benefit him in some way, it's not in his nature. She grabs the letter and reads it over again.

"**R**uth needs me and it's my turn to be there for her, like I should've always been." Eva smiles at her Mum.

"I kind of like this version of you better." Hannah smirks at her daughter's approval, she's always been there, just a little distracted for a while. Hannah talks into her phone. "Siri, find me the first one-way ticket to Poland!" Eva snatches the phone from her Mum.

"No Siri cancel that!" Hannah looks at Eva pleadingly, she needs to do this, but Eva has the biggest grin on her face. "Siri, find two one-way tickets to Poland!" Hannah nearly trips over herself and hugs Eva. There's no way she's not being part of the next chapter. "Looks like we're going on a Ruth Hunt," Eva sings into her Mum's ear.

L.A.GREENAN

Shibden Love & Money
Published by
Lindsey Armet-Greenan, 2023

Acknowledgement

The Shibden Valley, you inspired me, you haunted me, and I thank
you for the view. x
For all the many people who have accepted me, loved me, encouraged
me, despised me, belittled me, and abandoned me. Know your energy
has fed my creativity. So, thank you for the fuel. x
My circle of family and friends, you put up with me. And that is all I
could ever ask for. x
MK x
Coll. x
Keep learning, trying and most importantly believe in yourself. x

About the Author

L.A.Greenan is a Scottish creative based in Yorkshire.
Shibden Love & Money is her first book
Get in touch
Instagram: @l.a.greenan
Tik Tok: @lagreenan
Facebook: L.A.Greenan
Twitter: @lindseygreenan
Read more at lagreenan.com.